COVE

Book Four of The Scorpion Chronicles

Russell Turnbull

Russell Turnbull Studios

Russell Turnbull Studios
Carlisle, Pennsylvania

First Edition
Trade Paperback ISBN: 979-8989088539

Cover designed by Miblart.

THE SCORPION CHRONICLES

Hollow: Book One

Dark: Book Two

Vast: Book Three

Cove: Book Four

This book is for Corbin Beish.

You were right my friend, you were right.

CONTENTS

AUTHOR'S NOTES

Welcome back to the Realm of Beornan Heafod in this, the fourth installment to The Scorpion Chronicles Saga.

This was originally intended to be a trilogy, but I've fallen in love with these characters and have come up with even more interesting characters that I'm sure you'll fall in love with as well.

As with the preceding installments, you will undoubtedly find foreign words that you cannot translate easily.

They are either archaic words not used in today's languages, or (most likely) Olde French.

I have also mixed a bit of Irish, Gaelic and Latin (among other) words and terms within, because they fit their given situations and explain things a bit better than common English words and terms could.

If you find this confusing, I apologize in advance.

(You can use Google Translate to decipher almost everything within this saga.)

This book contains a lot of Afrikaans.

Chapter 7 translates into Scottish Gaelic.

It also translates into Afrikaans.

The characters Robin, Scarlett, John and Tuck are within the public domain.

I hope you enjoy this installment of The Scorpion Chronicles!

Russell Turnbull

THANKS

I would like to thank and/or mention the following:

My wife, Tania

Keri-Rae Barnum, New Shelves Books

Miblart, Ukraine

ERRFORDLAND

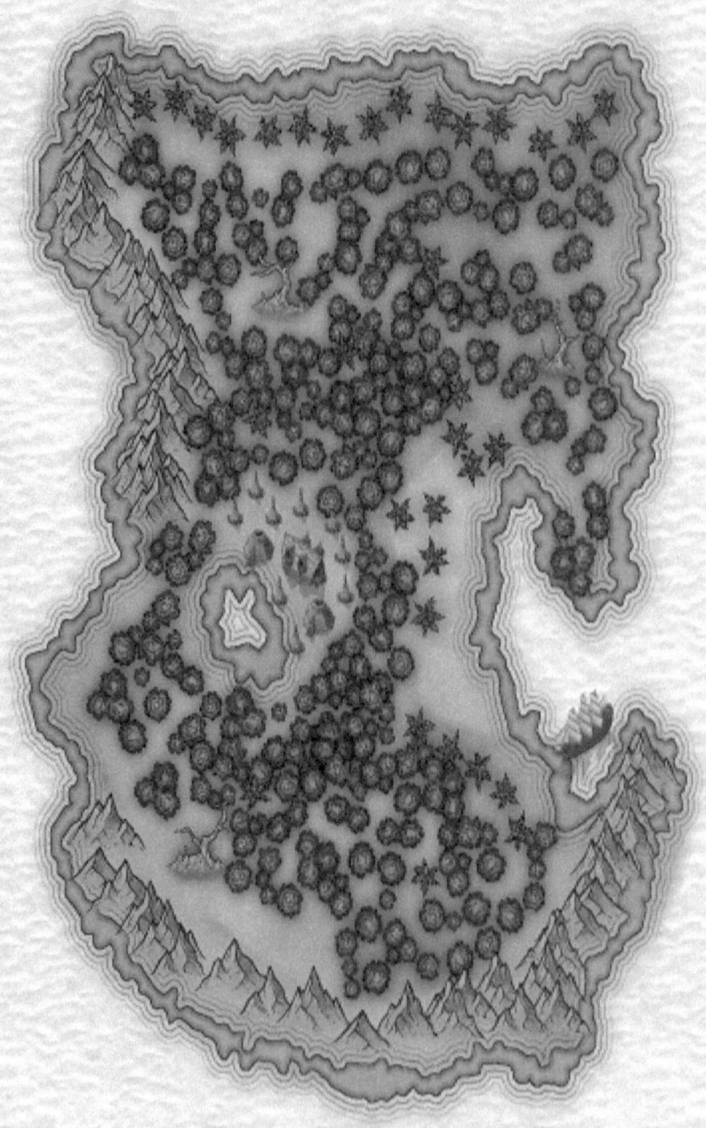

ILYN
<-- AVILYN HARBOR
HAZE MOUNTAIN
THE HAZE
EXLAND MOUNTAIN
THE SCORPION'S DEN
NTON
DEWARG
BOM DABO
<-- TO LARIX

PROLOGUE

"That was such a moving ceremony," Meeka sniffed and hugged Loher.

"Thank you," I beamed, "I especially liked the light show at the end."

"Kuchoff and I had it planned for a few days," Meeka giggled.

"Light show?" Loher asked, "I thought that was part of the kiss!"

Meeka and I laughed and tapped the rims of our mugs to Loher's drink.

The night sky was as clear as glass, teeming with billions and billions of stars.

The moon was almost full, or perhaps it was waning, I couldn't be sure.

We were moving at a slower pace than normal, enjoying the warm summer breeze on our skin, and blowing through our hair.

A party was in full swing, complete with Kuchoff playing a lute and singing, trying his best to keep a tune.

Loher and I decided to sneak off alone for a while.

Before we could successfully sneak away, Balt caught us, "We're gonna go lookin' fer t'em escaped wizards tamarrow, right?"

"It's going to be difficult," Loher stated, "but, yes."

"Guid," Balt smiled, gazed at Loher's new ring for a moment, raised his mug of ale in our direction, "Mister an' Missus McLaaud," he slurred, and then half stumbled away, looking for Rion.

⁙

We finally found ourselves in the crow's nest, high above the rest of our companions.

The sea was so calm, we could barely feel the sway from the waves.

We could still hear Kuchoff performing, keeping our found family entertained.

People were singing along and laughing.

I could even hear Balt, slightly inebriated, trying to explain a fighting style to Rion, but the dwarf's accent gets thicker the drunker he gets, and it was becoming increasingly difficult for the shy eline warrior to understand.

We stood up there in the crow's nest, holding each other, enjoying the peace and calmness in silence.

"So, what was your favorite part," Loher asked after a while, with closed eyes as she smiled and felt the warm breeze drift around her.

"The moment you said, 'I do.'" I whispered into her ear.

Her smile widened and she gently let her head rest on my shoulder.

"Mine was when Nitch started snoring," she admitted in a giggle, her hand failing to hide it, "his timing was perfect."

I pulled her a little closer and held her a bit tighter as The Scorpion rounded a bend around a small island.

I noticed that the music had suddenly stopped playing and Meeka was frantically asking Kuchoff what was wrong.

Kuchoff didn't respond, he just sat there, lute in hand, but motionless.

The laughter and chatter of conversation slowed and stopped.

"We need to investigate," Loher stated and grabbed my hand.

The climb down from the crow's nest seemed like it took ages, even with gravity on our side.

By the time we arrived on the deck, Kuchoff had gotten up and moved to the side of the ship, peering out into the darkness.

A crowd began to gather near.

"Kuchoff, sweetheart," Meeka pled, "what's wrong? What's going on?

No answer.

He just stood there, as if he were waiting, looking for something.

"Oi!" Balt prodded as he gently nudged Kuchoff with his finger, "Boy-o, are ye okay?"

Nothing.

"Are ya seasick or sumptin'?" Balt asked, trying to get even a small reaction out of his friend.

No reaction.

Not even a blink.

Balt looked at Meeka and sadly shook his head as he gave the teenager some room.

"Should we just leave him alone?" A concerned sailor asked.

"I don't know," Meeka admitted, not breaking her gaze.

"I'll keep an eye on him, Ma'am," the sailor offered.

"That's generous of you," Meeka tried to smile, "I would appreciate the extra eyes."

"I'll be right back," the sailor announced, "I'll go get more men to help keep an eye on him."

"Thank you," Meeka sighed and returned her focus on Kuchoff.

The sailor ran off, calling out to his friends.

"I'm sure everything will be fine soon," Brother Fost commented, trying to keep Meeka calm.

Meeka smiled weakly, "I really hope you're right, Brother Fost," she sighed and leaned against the ship's railing.

Light conversations and a little bit of hushed laughter began as people began to enjoy the festivities once again.

A trio of sailors struck up another old sea shanty and some of our shipmates began to dance.

Moments went by as the sailors and Meeka tried to revive Kuchoff's attention, but all he would do was stand there and stare out to the pitch-dark sea.

Watching.

Waiting?

For what?

For who?

Unexpectantly, Roash let out a sudden hiss and extended her natural claws.

We all began to frantically look around for some sort of danger.

As if from out of nowhere, a dark ship, comparable in size to The Scorpion, appeared from the darkness.

I leaned closer to Loher, "Talk about perfect timing."

She wasn't very amused.

Dark figures could barely be seen standing at her bow; I counted four.

As the ship grew closer, Kuchoff began to climb up the railing.

Meeka tried to stop him but found herself paralyzed.

Unable to move, Meeka called out, "Kuchoff!"

At that exact moment, the entirety of the approaching ship, now only meters away, suddenly lit up with fiery torchlight, revealing double rows of large cannons, hundreds upon hundreds of well-armed and armored human warriors, orcs, hobgoblins, and ogres, as well as the identities of the four figures up front.

Three of them were the escaped wizards we had once captured in the other realm...

"Well," Balt belched, "t'is makes it a whole lot easier ta find 'em."

The fourth figure standing on the bow with the three escapees was a little more difficult to see...

Kuchoff stepped down from the railing, fighting to move, he slowly began to make his way back away from the railing, a horrified look, dripping from his face, when a female voice softly called out from the opposing ship, "Kuuuuchooooff..."

The frightened teenager seemed to gain a little bit more control as he drew his katana and fearfully cried out in terror, "MOM??"

Chapter One

FROM A CERTAIN POINT OF VIEW

"This should be interesting," Tybidon Trislee mused as he lowered his spyglass, "They're heading straight for The Scorpion."

"Are you sure it's The Scorpion?" Navari gasped with excitement.

"Large, golden, shaped like a giant scorpion," Tybidon scoffed and smiled, "you know, I'm not completely sure."

Navari frowned and realized her folly, "It's just, I've never seen The Scorpion before, I've only heard the stories."

"Here," Tybidon said and handed Navari the spyglass, "see for yourself."

Navari took the spyglass.

The Scorpion loomed larger, dancing with the waves.

The legendary ship was quite easy to spot in the ever-growing darkness due to the setting sun reflecting from her coat of golden paint.

The Grand Ascendancy's ship, however, was almost invisible in the dark as it began to slow down and move closer to a small island near Exland mountain.

A sudden burst of fire balls, lightning arcs and energy balls erupted into the air from the bow of The Scorpion, followed by loud cheering, clapping, and whistling, followed by music and poor singing.

Shortly, The Scorpion began to move in the general direction of the Grand Ascendency's hidden ship.

"They have no idea that the Grand Ascendency is there," Navari gasped, "we've got to warn them!"

"By the time we get there," Tybidon sighed, "it will already be too late."

Navari clenched a fist in determination, "Then we have to *help* them."

Tybidon nodded his head in agreement, "Let's go tell the others."

⋯⟨◊⟩⋯

Grephine Rina, a human female around the age of thirty, was the captain of The Dragonfly.

Dressed in thick leather armor covered by a long, thin, black wool jacket, she stood at five foot, three inches (163 cm) and weighed approximately one hundred thirty-five pounds (61.3 kg).

Shoulder length black hair whipped around her dark, suntanned face as the sails of her ship engorged with wind and pushed The Dragonfly into motion.

Captain Rina's First Officer was Commander Tybidon Trislee, a large human male around the age of twenty-seven.

He was dressed from shoulder to toe in rough looking, blood-stained scale mail armor with pieces of banded armor affixed in places to help hold it together.

Short stubbly blonde hair covered his dented and scarred up scalp and ran down to an equally scarred up and offset jaw and chin.

His piercing blue eyes seemed to glow as he kept an eye on the Grand Ascendancy as The Scorpion sailed closer.

He stood around six foot, four inches (193 cm) and weighed more than two hundred fifty pounds (113.8 kg).

His weapon of choice was called, 'The Mourning Starr;' a self-made flail with an extra-long handle and a chain twice as long as it should be, normally.

Hanging from the end of the extra-long chain was a huge lump of blood-stained lead with spikes and blades jutting out of it.

It hadn't been cleaned in a while, or ever, and was beginning to stink.

Strips of skin and chunks of rotting flesh still clung to the massive wad of death.

It looked nasty, and I wouldn't even want to stand anywhere near it, let alone swing it around.

The crew's healer was a half human, half medusan of unknown age called Navari.

By all accounts, Navari looked like a human female, standing at five foot, four inches (162.5 cm) and weighing approximately 110 pounds (49.8 kg).

Navari's skin tone and complexion was comparable with Captain Rina's suntan, only Navari came by it naturally.

Navari's hair was indeed snakes of grey, brown and green, only mixed in and hidden within brown and greying human-like hair.

Navari's eyes...

The weapon of choice...

Navari's eyes were a great asset, as well as a downfall.

Purple in color, they mesmerized all who happen to gaze into them, causing the gazer to speak only their truth.

They also had the ability to turn someone to stone, temporarily or permanently.

Only the unfamiliar and truest of hearts dare to look upon Navari's face.

Dressed in a hooded cloak the color of moss, Navari's face, especially the eyes, were kept hidden under the hood from others.

The rest of the crew consisted of all adult humans of all genders and races, mostly fighters and archers, a few with basic magical abilities.

A rag-tag crew of misfits and fortune seekers, banded together for convenience, the love of adventure, and not much more.

<hr>

The Dragonfly sped as fast as the wind could take her toward the Grand Ascendancy's ship in hopes of getting there in time to stop whatever the evil faction was planning.

The Scorpion had disappeared behind one of the small islands for a moment, the music faded along with it, but then slowly came back into view; the cheerful music grew louder, and then gradually, sloppily, stopped.

Something was wrong.

Had the crew of The Scorpion seen the Grand Ascendancy's ship already?

How?

They were still hidden behind an island.

"Look!" Tybidon called, "Someone's climbing over the railing."

The crew of The Dragonfly gathered to see the spectacle unfolding as a few of the crew began to chant, "Jump... Jump... Jump..."

"Stow it." Captain Rina commanded as she walked out of her cabin.

The chanting stopped and the crew returned to their posts.

"Report." The captain barked.

"The Grand Ascendancy is taking position there, by Exland Mountain," Tybidon motioned, "The Scorpion seems to know that someone is out there, because the music stopped and that man is climbing over the railing, Captain."

"We're going as fast as the wind will take us," Navari added.

"They're up to no good, I agree," the captain commented in thought, "but what could they want with the mighty Scorpion of all ships?"

"With all due respect, Captain," Tybidon laughed, "they're only stories."

"We shall see in due time, Commander," Captain Rina smiled and watched as The Scorpion sailed past the Grand Ascendancy's darkened ship.

"I hope not," Navari groaned.

⸺⬦⸺

Without warning, The Grand Ascendancy's ship began to glow with firelight as dozens of torches suddenly burst into flames.

The Scorpion stopped.

No motion, except for the waves.

The two ships were now side to side.

The Dragonfly began to slow down and position herself mere meters from The Scorpion and her foe.

"Kuuuuuchoooooffff," a female voice sang out from one of the ships.

"What does *that* mean?" Navari asked.

Tybidon shrugged and shook his head.

"MOM?" The man on the railing suddenly called out and began retreating over the railing, and onto the deck, drawing his weapon.

"Kuchoff!" The woman's voice cried from aboard the Grand Ascendancy's ship, "I've been looking for you for years. I'm so glad you're alive. Where were you? Where's your father? I have so many questions..."

"NO!" Kuchoff shouted with obvious fear in his voice, "Go away and leave us alone!"

"Please, Kuchoff," the woman begged, "I've been searching for you and your father for so long, where is he?"

"He's *dead*," Kuchoff spat, "no thanks to you."

Navari gasped.

"Dead? How?" His mother asked, apparently in shock.

Tybidon leaned against the railing and took a swig from his canteen.

"Do you really care?" Kuchoff asked, apparently calmer now, "You had hobgoblins attack our town and made us believe you'd been captured or killed, now I see you being friendly with a hoard of them as well as the three men that have been attacking us for years, you have my crewmates frozen in place, why should we trust you? Why should *I* trust you?"

"I wouldn't," Tybidon commented.

Captain Rina agreed.

"Because I'm your mother," she said, "and you should always trust your mother."

"Blood isn't necessarily family," Tybidon commented again, drawing another agreement from the captain.

"No!" Another female voice screamed, **"I'm his mother!** You're just the bitch that birthed him."

"Ohhh..." Tybidon half groaned, half laughed.

A volley of energy balls suddenly burst from The Scorpion's deck and impacted on something (or someone?) on the opposing deck.

The stars suddenly dimmed as thousands of arrows from the Grand Ascendancy's ship darkened the already dark sky.

The Scorpion was pelted with a blanket of arrows that somehow harmlessly bounced off and fell into the sea.

"I didn't see *that* coming," Tybidon chuckled in surprise and involuntarily glanced at the captain.

Captain Rina smiled and winked at him in a knowing way.

Tybidon's smile quickly faded.

"Look!" Navari gasped and pointed at The Scorpion.

The legs of The Scorpion suddenly began to move, turning the ship in such a way that she swiftly brought herself around to face the port side of the enemy ship.

"They're only stories," the captain mocked her First Officer, laughed once again, and walked away.

The Scorpion's claws reached out and grasped ahold of the enemy ship, tipping it on its side, spilling its contents.

"Fire!" Captain Rina ordered.

The Archers aboard The Dragonfly began to peg off the confused foes that were suddenly dumped into the ice-cold sea.

The Scorpion's tail suddenly struck forward, between her sails, smashing through the hull of its prey, splitting the wooden ship in two.

Tybidon's eyes widened "If I didn't see it with my own two eyes..."

I could finally see the face of the figure standing with the three escaped wizards.

A woman, around forty years old stepped forward.

"Please, Kuchoff," his mother begged, "I've been searching for you and your father for so long, where is he?"

Kuchoff spun around to face the enemy ship, "He's **dead**," Kuchoff spat, "no thanks to you."

"Dead? How?" she asked, a smile of both triumph and relief etched upon her lips.

"Do you really care?" Kuchoff asked, calmer now, "You had hobgoblins attack our town and made us believe you'd been captured...or killed," he stepped closer to the railing, "now I see you being friendly with a hoard of them as well as the three men that have been attacking us for years," he motioned behind him with a wide arc of his hand, "you have my crewmates frozen in place, why should we trust you? Why should *I* trust you?"

"Because I'm your mother," she said with a wave of her hand, "and you should always trust your mother."

I could move again.

The King!

"No!" Meeka finally screamed, "**I'm his mother!** You're just the bitch that birthed him."

With no warning, Meeka fired off a volley of energy balls she had been charging, the whole time she was frozen, all at once, striking Kuchoff's mother directly in the chest, knocking her out of sight.

I must protect the King...

The stars suddenly dimmed as thousands of hobgoblin arrows darkened the nighttime sky.

My wife...

The King...

Who do I…

The Scorpion was pelted with a blanket of arrows that harmlessly bounced off from Nitch's natural defenses.

…protect?

The legs of The Scorpion suddenly began to move, turning the ship in such a way that she swiftly brought herself around to face the port side of the enemy ship.

"Kuchoff?" Balt called out in excitement, "Are ye dooin' t'is?"

Her claws reached out and grasped ahold of the bow and the port railings, tipping the ship on its side.

Hobgoblins, orcs, and humans alike, began to fall overboard and swim for their lives in the ice cold, shark infested darkness.

"No," Kuchoff called back, still in shock at what he had just experienced.

The Scorpion's tail suddenly lashed forward, between her sails, smashing through the hull of The Grand Ascendancy's ship, splitting it in two.

Balt and Kuchoff began to laugh hysterically as The Scorpion's tail retracted back, as if ready for another strike.

"If t'at's na ye dooin' it," Balt laughed…

The ship's double rows of heavy cannons allowed it to sink quickly, drowning most that were trapped inside.

Balt couldn't complete his question since he found the irony of the deadly, heavy cannons weighing the enemy ship down so hilarious, he could do nothing but laugh.

"Ja play wit De Scorpion, ja bound ta get stung, Mon," Captain Waxx stated factually.

Balt was bouncing with glee at the discovery of his new second favorite weapon.

Everyone on board was either cheering or in shock and disbelief.

"Fire!" a distant female voice called, followed by the sounds of bow strings snapping and arrows impacting soft, wet flesh.

Captain Waxx and some crew that were nearby began to move toward the sound.

"Wot ta?" Balt stammered in half laugh and followed the crowd.

Chapter Two

UNCERTAINTY

Kuchoff was frantically searching over the side of The Scorpion, looking for the body of his mother.

The rest of us were looking for her as well, while investigating the sounds of archers, also over the side of the ship.

"Kuchoff," Meeka pled, "please don't..."

"I'm not angry with you, if that's what you mean," Kuchoff reassured the wizard with a half-smile and a hug, and then continued searching, "I would have killed her myself, had I the chance."

Sharks began to tear the bodies apart, living, and dead.

"But she's your mother," Meeka argued over the cries of the enemy being torn apart.

"No." Kuchoff stated with a finger in the air, "No. You said it yourself. You're my mother. She's just the..."

Meeka stopped him with a tight hug.

"You didn't happen to see a human woman, did you?" I called down to the other, smaller ship.

"No," the female voice called from across, "but we'll keep a weather eye out."

"We want her alive, if possible," Kuchoff called over.

"Understood," the voice called back.

"Alive?" Meeka asked in slight disbelief.

"Alive," Kuchoff repeated, "so I can kill her myself and make sure she's dead."

An arrow impacted into an orc's head with a wet smack that was quickly followed by blood curdling screams of pain.

"Besides leaving you as a child, with your father to care for you," Meeka began, "she must have done something else to you to make you feel this way."

"Not to me," Kuchoff sighed as he leaned over the edge to get a better view, "to my father."

A frenzied shark suddenly leapt up toward Kuchoff but fell short by quite a long distance.

Kuchoff grinned a toothy grin.

"I don't understand," Meeka admitted.

Kuchoff slid down off the railing and began to slowly stroll toward the others, "Think about it," he began, "she married him and had a child with him, she grew a family with him, he was in love with her, and then one day, a few years later, she apparently stages a hobgoblin attack so she can what? Escape? From what? From whom?" He stopped and kicked a dead rat into a corner before continuing, "Then she leaves him. With a child."

The inhuman screams of fear and pain were quickly subsiding as our new, apparent friends picked off the last of the enemy.

Again, he stopped and looked her in the eyes, "He thought she was dead, and he had this child to raise on his own. I'm sure I was a lot to handle, with my Psy skills, but the fact that he thought she was dead and she wasn't..."

"Meeka, Kuchoff," Loher called as the magical duo approached, "this is the captain and crew of The Dragonfly," she offered.

Without warning, a large puff of orange smoke appeared near the King and his guards as a tall, robed figure stepped out and swiftly moved toward the King.

His men didn't react.

Frozen?

Brother Fost quickly fired three Holy Bolts at the figure, but they never found their target.

The smoke dissipated, revealing Avilyn, the old hoary elf from 'The Broken Blade.'

He was holding the priest's Holy Bolts in his hand, smiling at the halfling.

"His Majesty has been out long enough," Avilyn suddenly boomed, and the orange smoke once again began to grow and swirl around the elf, the King, and his men.

"Wait!" the King cried and stepped out of the smoke, "I feel as if you saved my life," he said to Captain Waxx and Meeka, "Come to the castle as soon as you can, I would like to reward you."

"All of us," Meeka asked, "or just us?"

"All of you," he smiled and stepped back into the fading smoke, "we'll christen The Scorpion with my flag and everything!"

The King noticed a frown of concern on the pirate captain's face, "A small flag? A simple banner," the King compromised until Captain Waxx stopped frowning, "yes, a small banner."

The smoke began to rise once again until we heard the pop.

They were gone, and Brother Fost's Holy Bolts were sitting on the deck in front of his bare feet.

"I wonder what my honeymoon is going to be like," Loher chuckled and nudged Roash into a giggle.

"Look what t'e cat dragged in," Balt roared out in laughter as Rion was literally dragging the wizard, Lemac across the deck toward the team.

Lemac was struggling to get away.

"I found this one trying to escape. Again," Rion purred and held his prey up, "can I eat him, or do you want him alive?"

"**Alive!**" The female voice called from The Dragonfly.

"They've been destroying towns and villages for no apparent reason," a deep male voice called out, "so we've been trailing them for years, and we want answers."

Meeka stepped closer to the railing and looked down at the smaller ship, "They've been attacking *us* for years as well," she called down.

"Then our aims are aligned," Captain Rina confidently called back up, "where shall we meet to interrogate him?"

"South Port Royal," Captain Waxx answered, "we have business d'ere."

"We should take him to the King," I called down.

"I should be there," a cloaked figure hissed up with a raspy voice.

"Yes," Captain Rina agreed, "Navari will be more helpful than you could ever dream of."

"We're headed there now," Meeka called down.

"Alright," Captain Rina agreed, "we'll follow you."

"You and you," Captain Waxx picked out two sailors, "take dat scum to de brig and stay d'ere until we get to de port."

⸺◈⸺

Kuchoff and Meeka kept an eye out for the body of his mother as The Scorpion and The Dragonfly pulled away from Exland Mountain and sailed in the direction of Dewarg.

Her body was never found, convincing Kuchoff that his mother was somehow still alive.

"It's inconceivable," Meeka sighed as she turned away from the railing, "three high powered energy balls, right into her chest. How could she survive that?"

"Maybe you vaporized her," Kuchoff suggested with a twinge of hopefulness.

"No," Meeka frowned, "it all just seems too easy. I think you're right, Kuchoff, I don't think we've seen the last of her."

A sailor had walked up a moment before, and patiently waited for a chance to politely interrupt them, "Ma'am," he respectfully began, "Captain Waxx requests your presence on the bridge."

"Escort me?" The wizard requested.

"This way, Ma'am."

"I'm going to go find Balt," Kuchoff laughed, "Ma'am."

Meeka smiled and shrugged her shoulders as the sailor escorted her to the bridge.

Moments later, they arrived at the bridge.

"The bridge, Ma'am," the sailor motioned to a door and then excused himself and walked away.

"Please come in," Captain Waxx offered.

"I've never been on the bridge of a ship before," Meeka stated and slowly looked around.

"I hope you'll get used to it," Captain Waxx smiled shyly.

Meeka suddenly looked worried and confused.

She had no interest in a relationship, but didn't know how to tell him...

"Oh! Nothin' like dat," the captain nervously laughed and took a step back, "I'd like to make you de First Officer of De Scorpion."

The worry on Meeka's face vanished, only to be replaced by more confusion.

"Honorary, of course," Captain Waxx clarified.

"Why?" Meeka asked, "I mean, why me?"

"You saved De Scorpion last night," the captain answered soberly, "we were all frozen, and I thought we were all goners."

"I was trying to save Kuchoff," Meeka admitted, "and besides, it was Nitch's energy dome that blocked all of the arrows."

"Dis is yet two more reasons, yor honesty and integrity, for me to ask again," the captain smiled, "do you accept?"

"What does it entail?" Meeka asked, becoming curious.

The captain smiled wider and chuckled, "nothing really, only yor word will be law, like mine."

"So, if I give your men an order, they'll follow it?" Meeka asked.

"Aye," Waxx nodded, "as if yor words were my own."

"Let me think on it."

"It's already been done," He smiled, "de crew took a vote dis morning, and de 'aye's' won by a landslide."

"So, this was the crew's idea?" she asked, blushing.

"Aye, an' I agreed wid' it." The captain smiled.

"Well," Meeka smiled shyly, "that explains the sudden politeness out there."

※

South Port Royal was bustling with people of all goodish races.

The sun was warm, and the air smelled of strong salt and a bit like dead fish.

The Scorpion was ushered into a secure mooring area by two Royal Guards.

"Ahoy," a guard called out, "we've been expecting you."

"Ahoy," a sailor called back, "permission to disembark?"

"Granted," the guard affirmed, "welcome to Salvus Hus."

The crew of The Scorpion rapidly set to their tasks of securing The Scorpion, while Captain Waxx led the rest of us off the ship.

"We should go find Captain Rina and her ground team," I suggested.

"Over there," Rion called as he picked up his prisoner, the wizard, Lemac, off the ground and slung him roughly over his shoulder.

Lemac let out a painful grunt, "Easy, Fleabag."

"I'll eat you," Rion threatened.

"Awe," Balt whined, "an' yer na gonna share wit' me?"

"Raw," Rion purred and smiled at the dwarf.

"Now I don't want any," Balt teased.

"Let's get going you two," Roash laughed and led the way.

Captain Rina and Commander Trislee of The Dragonfly met us near the dock where they moored.

They were accompanied by the strange, cloaked figure called Navari.

"You get a private dock?" Captain Rina quipped as she reached out and shook Captain Waxx's hand.

Captain Waxx only shook his head, and her hand and said, "Dis be de first time."

"I'm Captain Rina, and this is my First Officer, Commander Trislee, and our resident healer, Navari."

"I'm Captain Waxx, and my First Officer, Meeka Ashpin," he motioned toward the wizard.

"Wot?" Balt asked for the rest of our team.

Meeka blushed and tried to look commanding, "We'll explain later."

"Another wedding?" Brother Fost sighed, "so soon?"

"No," Captain Waxx and Meeka sternly corrected together.

"The rest of us will introduce ourselves later, I'm sure, but if you don't mind," I added, "we should take our prisoner to the King at once."

Rion growled in agreement.

The two Royal Guards attempted to relieve Rion of his burden, but Rion just roared loudly at them, and they quickly backed off.

"With all due respect, Captain Waxx," Tybidon nervously laughed, "I always thought the stories about The Scorpion were just that... stories."

Captains Waxx and Rina only smiled at each other and began following the guards to the castle.

"Do you already know each other?" Kuchoff asked.

"Only in passing," Captain Rina answered, "aren't you a little young to be away from home?"

"Kuchoff here, is far more than he seems," Meeka proudly informed.

"So is Navari," Commander Trislee laughed and motioned to the cloaked figure.

The castle seemed to grow the closer we drew to it.

Carts of goods and wares were being pulled by horses of all sizes and breeds.

Roash and Rion were fascinated.

"Have you never seen a horse before?" Navari asked.

"Never this close," Roash gleamed.

"They're usually afraid of us," Rion chuckled.

"I've been noticing a lot of fearful looks from the people around here," Roash purred.

"Fearful?" Brother Fost asked, "I'd say more like...curious."

"I'd say, uncertainty," I commented.

We walked along the packed dirt trail for a few more moments, "I can already hear a pint er four callin' me name," Balt sang as we passed through the Royal gates.

"King first, drink later," Rion growled.

"Ye really wanna eat t'is guy, huh?" Balt swallowed hard and feigned a laugh.

Rion just licked his teeth and kept walking in silence, while the horrified Lemac began to tremble.

"E's na really gonna eat 'im, is 'e, Roash?" Balt asked, growing more uneasy.

Roash leaned closer to the prisoner's face and extended her natural claws, glaring at the captive wizard.

Suddenly, Rion began to softly laugh, "Why did you do that Roash?" Rion moaned, "He just pee'd on me."

CHAPTER THREE

AND THE TRUTH SHALL...

The throne room was exactly how I remembered it.

King Lagu Ofer'Eal was seated on his throne as we entered.

"Don't bow to the King," I whispered to the group, "he hates formality."

"Clearly, you're joking," Captain Rina laughed.

"He's serious," Brother Fost vouched.

"Just follow my lead," Captain Waxx confirmed.

As we approached the throne, Avilyn, the old hoary elf appeared next to the King and sat down on the secondary throne.

Commander Trislee gasped in awe at the spectacle.

"You don't get out much, do you Commander?" I quipped at his reaction.

He just looked at me with a grin and rubbed his scarred head as if to say, 'I've seen some action.'

"Welcome, Friends," the King chimed, and then noticed the ragdoll slung over Rion's shoulder, "what do we have here?" he asked as he rose from his seat and greeted us.

"A criminal and his victims, Your Majesty," Brother Fost announced.

"Which is the criminal?" The King asked rhetorically, looking directly at Lemac.

Rion growled and tossed Lemac to the floor like a ragdoll.

Lemac landed hard with a bone crunching thud in front of the King; he let out a stifled groan and laid there, motionless, in fear of Rion.

"I see..." The King observed, stifling a giggle, "...and the victims?"

The rest of us raised our hands.

The King was genuinely shocked, "You've been busy," he said to Lemac, "rise if you can."

"I do not dare, my Liege," Lemac shivered.

"And why is that?" The King asked.

"That monster will eat me," Lemac whimpered.

Rion growled for effect.

"Is this true?" The King asked with a skeptical smile.

"I'm hungry," Rion purred menacingly, not confirming nor denying a thing.

The smile dropped from the King's face, "I see," he frowned.

"I know of this man," Avilyn announced and strode to the King's side, "he *is* a criminal. And a liar; don't believe a word he says until proven accurate."

Lemac scowled at Avilyn.

Avilyn sneered back.

"I can help with that," Navari hissed and took a few steps forward.

"And you are?" the King asked, curious.

"I am called Navari," the cloaked figure answered, "I have the ability, among others, to draw the raw truth from any intelligent being."

"How fortunate!" Avilyn exclaimed, "The Grand Ascendancy has a lot to answer for. No better place to start than here and now."

"You know of The Grand Ascendancy?" Kuchoff asked in surprise.

The old hoary elf just looked back at the psyonisist with a blank, emotionless look on his face.

"How do you do it, Navari?" the King asked, growing increasingly excited.

"With your permission," Navari requested.

The King rolled his eyes at the formality, "By all means," he prompted.

"Commander," Navari coaxed.

Tybidon walked over and grabbed up Lemac from the floor, spun him around and gripped the wizard's face from behind, propping his eyes open.

Navari stood in front of Lemac and opened her hood, finally showing her face.

"Y.. you're.. you're a medusan!" The King gasped and quickly turned away, shielding his Royal face.

"Don't look at her!" I yelled and pulled Loher closer, shielding her face with my own.

Navari began to laugh, "It's alright, just don't look me in the eyes," she stated, "but *you will*," she hissed at Lemac, grabbed his face, and began to metaphorically dive deep into his soul.

"What do we want to know?" Captain Rina asked the room.

Kuchoff was the first to speak, "Is Amaliya Magnus still alive?"

"Who?" Balt whispered.

"His mother, you idiot," Meeka hissed.

"I t'ought t'at *you* was his mot'er," Balt whispered back in confusion.

Meeka shook her head in bewilderment, "Hush now," she scolded.

"Is Amaliya Magnus still alive," Navari repeated to Lemac.

"Yes," Lemac answered with no emotion or hesitation.

"How?" Meeka asked, stunned, "I hit her directly in the chest with three energy balls."

"She was never aboard our ship," Lemac answered stoically, "she projected herself psionically from the top of Exland Mountain. You hit Granier in the chest with your three energy balls."

"Who was Granier?"

"My former master."

"Why is The Grand Ascendancy after us?" I asked, yet I was sure that I already knew the answer.

"Amaliya wants her son to join The Grand Ascendancy," Lemac answered as red smoke began to swirl around him and before anyone, including Commander Trislee or Avilyn could react, the prisoner escaped once again.

"Dammit!" Rion roared.

"You *were* gonna eat 'im!" Balt gasped.

"How did he escape?" The King stomped angrily.

"I shall investigate, my Liege," Avilyn assured as he too, puffed away in a cloud of orange smoke.

"Someone rescued him," Meeka stammered, "I made absolutely sure he had no magical objects, trinkets or baubles on his person."

"You are correct, Meeka," Navari assured as she hid her face beneath her hood once again, "he was in a trance, mentally under my control and unable to perform magic. Someone indeed, rescued him."

"Probably my mother," Kuchoff scowled and punched the air.

"Well," I sighed, "at least we know for sure that she's still alive."

"And she's probably not going to give up," Brother Fost added.

"The attacks are probably going to get worse, more frequent," Roash guessed.

There came a familiar POP from the other side of the room as Avilyn appeared in a puff of orange smoke, "The Grand Ascendancy is, in fact, sailing past my harbor as we speak," he reported, "it looks as though they are preparing to turn toward the Haze."

"I wish we could follow them," Kuchoff breathed, "and find out where they're based."

"Why can't we?" The King asked.

We all stopped and looked at him.

"We should go to the Haze and find them," his Majesty formulated, "and while we're in the Haze, I can give you your reward!"

"I cannot allow..." Avilyn began.

"Avilyn," the King interrupted, "you're coming with us."

"As you wish, Sire," Avilyn reluctantly agreed, "under protest."

"Well now," the King said and clapped his hands together, making a loud smack, "we have festivities and rewards to award," he smiled brightly and looked around from face to face, "shall we?"

POP!

Avilyn's orangish smoke quickly faded away in the gentle breeze coming from the sea.

The Scorpion loomed before us.

All the previous damage was repaired, but the paint was no longer fully gold.

"What have they done to my ship?" Meeka gasped without realizing what she had said.

Captain Waxx smiled from ear to ear, overjoyed in the knowledge that Meeka had accepted her 'promotion' as First Officer, "I had de crew paint 'er more...natural colored so she won't stand out so much in de dark."

The shiny gold paint had been replaced with dull browns, greens, and reddish tones.

The Scorpion looked more like an actual scorpion now.

Her bright sails had also been replaced with dull bluish grey.

"How *did* you get The Scorpion to crawl and sting like that," I asked, "magic?"

"That was amazing!" Loher agreed.

"I t'ought it was Kuchoff," Balt added.

"So did I," Brother Fost admitted.

Kuchoff half-smiled and shook his head.

"Follow me," Captain Waxx suggested as he led the way aboard, "I show you."

We boarded the ship and were led down to the hold, past our quarters and into the center of the lower deck.

"Ja see dat little peg on de mast?" the captain asked.

We all agreed that we could see it.

He reached over and pulled the peg from its hole.

A small contraption suddenly sprung up from the floor.

It looked like a horse saddle with two cranks below it, apparently for use by the feet of the operator.

Above the saddle was a small ship's steering wheel and a periscope.

Beside the saddle were two levers, one on each side.

He didn't explain exactly how it worked, but we now knew that it was possible.

"We call it de creature controls," the captain laughed.

The captain stepped on a button and the whole contraption suddenly disappeared back into its resting position, secured by the peg being returned to its hole, "And d'ere ja be," he said and began to walk back to the upper deck.

"If we're heading out to find Kuchoff's mother," Captain Rina began, "should we follow in The Dragonfly, or stay aboard The Scorpion?"

"I really wish we wouldn't call her that," Kuchoff stated, "Meeka is my mother, and I'll have a go at anyone who says different."

"What should we call her then?" I asked.

"We could just call her, 'Amaliya'," Nitch finally spoke up.

"That'll do," Kuchoff half-smiled.

"Okay, fine," Captain Rina sighed, "should we follow in The Dragonfly..."

"Aye," Captain Waxx agreed, cutting his counterpart off, "follow in De Dragonfly. Dat way we have more firepower."

"Agreed," Captain Rina nodded and nudged Commander Trislee to follow her.

"I'm going to stay aboard The Scorpion," Navari announced, "I may be of more help here."

Captain Rina nodded acknowledgment and deboarded The Scorpion.

"Let me show you to your quarters, Majesty, Avilyn, Navari," Meeka offered and led the way back down to the hold.

Navari, the King, and Avilyn followed the First Officer and disappeared around a corner.

"How are you doing, Kid?" I finally asked Kuchoff now that we had a chance to breathe.

"I'm angry," he answered.

"Understandable," Loher comforted.

"And scared," Kuchoff admitted.

"I think most of us are as well," Roash stated.

"I'm not," Rion purred.

"Me neit'er," Balt chuckled, "why ain't we movin'?"

Just then, as if on cue, The Scorpion lurched into motion.

Moments later, both ships were sailing up the river towards Avilyn Harbor and on their way to the Haze.

"Avilyn," Kuchoff asked, "why is everything named after you?"

"The Strait of Avilyn, Avilyn Harbor and even the King of Dragons?" Avilyn listed.

"Right," Kuchoff agreed, curious.

"Well," the old hoary elf began, "I have been the Royal Magician for oh, since His Majesty's great, great, great, great... I lose track sometimes, but I have been in service to the last sixteen Kings."

"That's a long time," the King and Kuchoff gasped together.

"I'm very old," Avilyn chuckled.

"How old are you??" Kuchoff asked in disbelief.

"Kuchoff!" Meeka scolded.

Avilyn laughed, "Old enough to have owned the entire Desert Dunelands before the Dragon War."

"But *my* family owns the half that Guadium sits on," Meeka retorted.

"This, I know, my dear," Avilyn smiled, "I gifted the only useful land to one of your ancestors, long ago."

"Really?" Meeka asked, "why?"

"He was a powerful ally of mine," Avilyn answered, "an immensely powerful wizard, almost as powerful as me. But not quite."

"What was his name?" Meeka asked with genuine curiosity.

"Drake Ashpin," Avilyn replied after a moment of thought.

"Drake Ashpin," Meeka became lost in thought.

"Did he save your life?" The King asked.

"He saved *millions* of lives," Avilyn remembered, "but that is a story for another time."

A small cheer suddenly arose from near the main mast as the King's banner was hoisted into place.

Captain Waxx didn't look completely thrilled with the new addition to his ship, but when the King makes a decision, there's not much that can be done to change it...right away.

"Now that *that's* done," the King announced, "you must take me to The Hollow that I had you explore several years ago. I want to explore."

"With all due respect, my Liege," Captain Waxx argued, "ain't we supposed ta be lookin' for Kuchoff's m... Amaliya?"

"In due time, Captain," the King sang as he looked over the railing at a pod of dolphins seemingly leading the way, "if she's out here, she'll find us, besides, I'm sure you'll love what happens when we get there."

"My Liege?" Captain Waxx questioned.

The King looked the captain in the eyes and smiled, "Trust me."

Confused, the captain nodded reluctantly and yelled, "Helm, take us to De Hollow."

"Aye Sir," the reply came.

"Kuchoff," the King called over, "come look at this!"

"I think you made a new friend," Meeka giggled.

"I think *he* needs one more than I," Kuchoff said as he stood up, "someone his own age, like me," Kuchoff smiled and walked away.

The two young men stood on the bow, looking over the railing, enjoying the companionship of someone within a few years of each other.

It was not only good for the King to associate with Kuchoff, but for Kuchoff, in the mental state he was currently in, it was life changing.

"SHIP AHOY!" The call came from the crow's nest, high above the deck.

We all looked up to see which way the scout was pointing.

Starboard.

"Is it Amaliya?" Meeka called up.

After a moment, "No, Ma'am," the scout called down, "she's flying Swapton colors!"

"Don't get complacent, Mates," a sailor called out, "Amaliya could be anywhere, including that ship."

"He's right," Kuchoff added, "it's highly doubtful she's on that very ship, but her men could be."

"Understood," a handful of sailors barked as the crew returned to their duties.

We kept an eye on the Swapton ship until it rounded the bend and headed toward the river.

"I think we all may be becoming paranoid," Brother Fost observed.

"Overly cautious," Balt corrected.

"Agreed," Roash hissed.

"Either way," Brother Fost announced, "it isn't good for our psyches, we need to either relax or take on a task."

"I choose relax until we get to wherever it is that we're going," Roash decided and stretched her body.

"Nap time," Rion purred and slunk off to his quarters.

"Awe, Mate," Balt complained after him, but the eline disappeared down the stairs.

"At least he was above decks while we're in motion," Roash purred and found a sunny spot near the harpoon.

"That's true!" Brother Fost rejoiced, and scampered off to who-knows-where.

"You're going to nap there?" I asked, astonished.

"I'm not napping," she yawned, "I'm just going to rest my eyes."

"She's nappin'," Balt grumbled, "come on McLaaud-s," he blinked at Loher and me, remembering we're now married, "let's go git some eats."

"I *am* kind of hungry, aren't you?" Loher admitted.

"I could eat," I agreed as we followed the dwarf to the mess hall.

Chapter Four

Is Anybody Home?

As we were passing through the Yfel Holh Cave area, we rounded the bend around Exland Mountain.

The Scorpion silently navigated through the waters of The Haze, as the captain called out orders to his crew, occasionally warning them to be careful of the submerged rocks below the water's surface.

A crew member leaned way over the railing of The Scorpion's bow, verbally guiding the helmsman through the many unseen rocks.

The Scorpion lightly bounced off rocks from time to time, but with no real damage done to the ship.

"I doubt anyone would be foolish enough to follow us in here," Loher stated as we once again bumped off another rock.

It was slow going for a while as The Scorpion had to literally tiptoe across water, too shallow to sail in, toward The Hollow.

Eventually, a small dock reached out to the ship from an island to the left and we could settle back down into the water.

The Dragonfly, a much smaller ship, was arriving through the rocky passage, seemingly unharmed.

The island itself was just a cropping of mountains that looked as if they were just floating motionless in the sea.

The Scorpion moored to the dock, now larger than it was the first time.

"I remember blinking everyone over to the island last time," Meeka giggled as she led the team to the island.

"I remember how frightened I was the first time we arrived," Brother Fost admitted.

"I remember t'e olyame!" Balt growled in joy.

"Olyame?" Rion questioned.

"Oh, t'ey're *fun*!" Balt squealed.

"I wonder if Bolla is still around," I thought aloud.

"Come on, come on," the King urged, "let's explore!"

Loher grabbed the King by the shoulder and spun him around to face her, "I'm only going to tell you this *once*, so you'd better pay attention," she said sternly, lightly shaking the King to get him to focus, "this is *not a game* and there *are* dangerous creatures in there. King or not, you *will* follow my orders."

The King smiled and nodded his head vigorously in agreement.

"I'm serious," Loher warned, "that goes for all of you!"

"So, I have to follow your orders?" I teased.

"Especially you," Loher snapped.

Avilyn just stood there in the background, smiling, relieved that the King took her command so well.

"Is she always like this?" Captain Rina asked Waxx.

"Dis be actually de first time I witnessed it, Mon..err..Ma'am."

Rina chuckled.

As we reached the mouth of the cave, we decided to take a short rest from the hour of climbing we had just accomplished.

"What is that *smell*?" Meeka asked in disgust, waving the air around in front of her nose.

"Yes, what *is that?*" Brother Fost commented, pinching his nostrils together with a thumb and forefinger.

"I think it smells good," Rion purred, "it's his weapon," he said, pointing to Commander Trislee's Mourning Starr, still caked in its last victim's flesh.

"Awe, Buddy," Balt cried in horror at the sight of the weapon, "I t'ought yer armor was bad, but t'at weapon o' yers 'as *got* ta be cleaned and sharpened. An' ye might as well take off t'at armor, I'm gonna fix t'at too."

"I guess we're staying for a while," I laughed and handed my blades and chest plate to Balt.

"Here, Balt," Loher sighed and handed him her longsword, "you might as well sharpen mine too."

"Hand 'em over," Kuchoff laughed as he too, handed his katana to the dwarf, "all of you. Blades and metal armor."

"Will we be safe?" Rina asked, "After Loher's warning..."

"You'll be fine," Avilyn spoke, "Kuchoff will cover us with a Psy Dome if needed."

"You know about that?" Kuchoff asked, surprised.

The old hoary elf just looked again at the psyonisist with a blank, emotionless look on his face.

"I'll start a fire," Brother Fost gleefully announced and set to his normal camping tasks.

Captain Rina and Commander Trislee handed their weapons to Balt.

"Yer armor too, Trislee," Balt urged as he inspected the carnage still stuck on the Mourning Starr.

Captain Rina smiled and nodded a silent order to her First Officer.

Reluctantly, the commander began to remove his broken, mismatched, dirty armor and toss the heap at the happy dwarf's feet.

Balt immediately set to work by the already roaring fire, scraping and hammering away.

We sat by the fire, sharing food, drink, new stories, and fond memories; getting to know our new companions.

One by one, we settled in for the night, awaiting our upcoming adventure.

⚔

We awoke to what looked like brand-new weapons and armor neatly laid out in a row.

Balt was snoring in a pile of rocks.

"How can he sleep like that?" The King yawned.

The snoring stopped, "I'm a dwarf, yer Majesty," Balt answered without opening his eyes, "we're raised t'is way."

"Interesting," the King murmured.

Balt's snoring continued.

"Between Balt's snoring and the eline's purring all night," Loher laughed, "I'm surprised anyone slept."

"I slept like a rock," Kuchoff grinned his famous toothy grin.

"Oi now," Balt snored at the pun.

Brother Fost, as usual, already had the fire stoked and a bit of food cooking.

Roash and Rion were stretching and scratching the sleep away, while the rest of us inspected our weapons and armor.

"Didn't you sleep, Loher?" Commander Trislee asked as he finished strapping the last, now clean, piece of armor to his leg.

"I rarely do," she commented, "we elves need very little sleep."

"Speaking of elves," the King said, looking around, "where's Avilyn?"

"I hope he didn't go into the Hollow alone," Loher gasped.

"Oh, I'm sure he didn't go far," Avilyn said, looking around a large rock, his forefinger pressed to his lips.

Loher immediately understood the jest and played along by obviously continuing the search.

"Who are we looking for?" I asked, still trying to wake up, wishing I had some coffee.

"Avilyn went missing," Avilyn teased and winked at me, still 'looking around' with everyone else.

"When was the last time..." I caught the joke and smiled at the elder elf, "...anyone saw him?"

Avilyn smiled back.

"We woke up and he was gone," the King answered, rubbing his eyes, frantically searching.

"We've *got* to find him!" Meeka urged, trying not to giggle.

After what seemed like twenty minutes, Avilyn finally stood directly in front of the King and cleared his throat, "perhaps you should've kept a better eye on him, m'Liege."

The King scowled and looked up at the elf, "It's not my..." he noticed who he was about to yell at and calmed down, "why must you plague me so?"

"Because I am the only one who can get away with it, Sire," Avilyn laughed and nudged the King in the arm.

We were all smiling as we packed up our gear and began to enter the Hollow.

The natural light coming from the mouth of the Hollow didn't reach extremely far, so we had to light a few torches.

"Are you sure our ships will be safe out there?" Captain Rina asked.

"They're going to meet us on the other side," Meeka giggled, "Captain Waxx is probably escorting The Dragonfly to the secret cove as we speak."

"It was supposed to be a surprise," Commander Trislee laughed, a bit disappointed.

"There's a *secret cove?*" The King asked in disbelief.

"You already know about it," Kuchoff chuckled, "Sire," he added.

The team rounded a curve and began to descend the tunnel.

The flickering from the torches was sending long, strange looking shadows in every direction.

"Perhaps we shouldn't address His Highness as royalty for the time being?" Avilyn suggested as he silently cast a light spell that drowned out the torches.

"Why not?" The King calmly inquired.

Balt quickly extinguished the lit torches so they wouldn't be wasted and stowed them in his pack.

"As not to draw unwanted attention from bandits and thieves who might be lurking within," the magician explained and scanned the immediate area with his eyes.

The two younger men nodded in agreement.

The tunnel gradually became wider the further down the team went.

"What should everyone address me as instead?" The King asked.

"I always liked the name, Rich," Brother Fost announced.

Nitch giggled from inside the priest's hood, "Sounds like Nitch."

"Too fitting," Rion argued.

The sound of rushing water could be faintly heard, growing louder the deeper we went.

"How about, Gavin?" Meeka suggested.

The King frowned, "Too...peasant-y," he complained.

"Then it's *perfect*." Avilyn decided.

"Gavin it is," Kuchoff agreed and slapped his new friend lightly on the back.

"Then perhaps I should have my own weapon," Gavin stated.

"Can you fight?" Rion growled as he stopped and looked at the young man.

"Yes," Gavin stated confidently and stood a bit straighter.

"What style?" Roash asked, suddenly showing interest.

"May I?" Avilyn offered.

Gavin nodded allowance.

"Gavin is proficient in archery, fencing, wrestling men his own size, and knife throwing."

"Knives, hey?" Navari hissed, "Impressive."

"I have some," Meeka offered, "don't lose them. I want them back as soon as you find yourself a replacement."

Gavin nodded in agreement.

She handed him her throwing knives as looks of confusion and awe washed over the faces of everyone except for Captain Rina, Commander Trislee and Navari, who didn't know Meeka as well as the rest of us.

"You had t'ose t'e whole time," Balt stammered, "an' I never knew it??"

"There's a lot about me you don't know," Meeka smiled.

"Are you sure you're comfortable using those?" Avilyn quietly asked.

"I'm sure," Gavin whispered back, "I just hope I don't need to, but I do feel safer and a little more in control now."

"That's important," Rion purred.

We continued deeper into the cave and reached the place Brother Fost had tossed his coin over the edge.

We never heard it hit bottom.

"Oi, Fost," Balt chuckled, "ye wanna toss anot'er one?"

"Perhaps Gavin would like to," the priest suggested and handed a coin to the new adventurer.

"What do I do with this?" He asked and turned the coin over in his hand.

"Toss it over the edge and count how long it takes to hit the bottom," Kuchoff instructed.

Gavin steadied the coin on his thumb and then gave it a flick.

TING!

The coin sang in the air.

Its song fading away the further it fell...

The further it fell...

It fell...

Fell...

...

Gavin's eyes widened as he strained to hear, "there's nothing down there!"

"Or it landed in water," Avilyn smugly guessed.

"Hmm..." Brother Fost voiced, "Why didn't *I* think of that?" He paused for a moment, thinking, "Well, either way, no, not water."

"I was hoping you would say, 'lucky guess,'" Avilyn snorted.

We continued down the path, further into the dark void.

The ledge path began to narrow, herding us into a single file line against the wall.

"T'at's a looonng fall," Balt grimaced.

"Just be careful," I began, "try not to look down too often and go at your own speed."

"I'm na worried about meself, Mate," Balt laughed, "I'm worried about Meeka's t'rowing knives."

I rolled my eyes at the dwarf, "I said that more for the K...Gavin's benefit."

"What did I say?" Balt commented in confusion.

I shook my head and continued strafing the ledge.

"We really should install some sort of safety railing across there," Gavin breathed as he safely reached the other side.

We all conveyed our agreement and continued into the large cavern where we fought the Rackarn.

"I still smell burnt goo," Balt sniffed and snorted.

"I don't smell anything," Roash purred.

"Memories are a strange thing, Balt," Brother Fost chuckled.

I looked at the two tunnels branching left and right, a bit confused about which way to go, so I simply listened into each tunnel and chose the one that sounded like rushing water.

"This way," I stated and began down the path.

"What's the other way?" Gavin asked.

"A dead end," I answered, "literally."

Further down the ever-descending path, the air began to become humid, thick, and smelled metallic.

Little by little, we began to see pools of dried blood caked all over the walls, floor, and ceiling.

Scenes of terror etched into time.

"What happened in here?" Captain Rina asked with sudden alarm in her voice as she quickly drew her cutlass and looked around.

Commander Trislee and Kuchoff followed suit.

"T'e olyame," Balt replied with excitement and readied his Great Axe.

"They're fun?" Rion echoed Balt's earlier statement.

"You bet 'cha," Balt grinned.

"I hope Bolla is alright," I said to the room and strung up my bow, "I'm surprised we haven't seen him yet."

"Isn't that door I found, around the next turn?" Loher asked, "Perhaps he's in the cove."

"Maybe we should go there next," I suggested.

"I wish there was another way around," Loher commented.

As we stood in front of the secret door Loher had found years ago, Balt began to giggle like a wee dwarf.

"What's so funny?" Loher asked, amused.

"Monty's behind t'at door," Balt smiled, trying to become serious.

"That's why I wish there was another way around," Loher admitted as she successfully found the locking mechanism.

"I was about to remind you that the dragon is dead," Brother Fost added, "in case that was your reason."

"Did you seriously just say, 'dragon'," Commander Trislee quipped.

"Quite," the priest affirmed.

The commander's smile faded.

"Kuchoff killed it," Meeka proudly announced.

"I was nine at the time," Kuchoff stated.

"Six," Balt corrected, "an' we helped."

"Time flies by..." Kuchoff shrugged.

The pair of officers looked at Kuchoff in disbelief while Navari seemed a little bit more believing.

But who could tell as no one could see her face.

"Are we ready to go in?" Loher asked as the locks clicked open and the stone door began to move.

We all had our weapons ready, archers in the back.

"Balt," Loher said as she took her position beside me, our bows ready, "Would you like to do the honors?"

"Monty. Mate..." Balt chuckled as he began to push open the stone door, "If I have ta kill ye again, so be it."

"Is Monty the dragon?" Navari asked as she crouched down behind Loher.

"No," I whispered, "Kusagi was the dragon," I pulled slightly back on my bowstring as the door opened wider, "Monty was a Royal Soldier."

"Necromancy?" She asked.

I nodded affirmation and pulled back a little more.

"Please," Loher warned as the door completely opened, "don't touch *anything*."

Balt rushed into the room with a loud battle cry which ended abruptly.

Silence.

A moment lapsed as we began to slowly rise and start for the door.

"Ye might wanna come in 'ere an' look at t'is," Balt's voice was quiet.

We all filed quickly into the room, and as Avilyn entered, his light spell lit up the enormous chamber, now filled with all the pirate treasure as well as the dragon's hoard.

"That's a lot of treasure," Tybidon Trislee breathed in complete awe.

"Can we touch it now?" Gavin asked eagerly, eyeing a large gem.

"It be safe enough, Mon," Captain Waxx smirked as he entered the room from the opposite end, "besides, it all be yours, except for dis pile, dat's mine."

The King (Gavin) looked around at the enormous wealth that surrounded him.

"So thisss iss the new King," a familiar voice hissed.

"Bolla!" I cried in relief that my friend was still alive and (hopefully) well.

"I'm afraid I may have to correct you on something, Captain Waxx," the King sternly announced.

"Your Majesty?" The captain gulped.

"Not only did I put my banner on your ship," he stepped closer to the captain, pointing a finger at him, "but all of this treasure," he said raising his arms out and slowly spinning around to see the wealth, "is........" he paused for effect as the captain began to fume with anger, "yours, but you have to share it with your crew and friends here."

Captain Waxx was shocked.

"Do you see what happens when you save the King's life?" The King smiled and shook the pirate captain's hand.

"Congratulationss, friendss!" Bolla sang and grasped my hand.

"Why did you move everything in here?" I asked as Bolla greeted some of the others.

"Sso The Grand Asscendanssy couldn't find it by chanss," the Lacerta priest hissed, "they've been sslinking around looking for ssomeone."

"That would be me," Kuchoff smiled his normal toothy grin and waved.

"I remember you," Bolla smiled, "you were jusst a boy back then."

Kuchoff continued to smile.

"What a letdown," Rion growled.

"Rion!" Both Meeka and Roash snapped.

"You call this a letdown?" The King gasped.

"I t'ink what me friend 'ere is let down wit' is," Balt laughed nervously and stepped between the eline and the King, "we didn't git ta kill no olyame, yer Highness."

"No Monty either," Rion added.

"I gots ta admit, I'm feelin' a wee bit let down meself."

The King smiled and said, "I understand, friends, the treasure means less than the fight."

"T'e treasure is guid, yer Honor," Balt stammered, "guid treasure."

"We eradicated the olyame a few yearss ago," Bolla announced proudly, "now we only ssee them in other cavess."

"This was a fun adventure, your Majesty," Avilyn remarked, "but I feel that our time has come to return to the castle."

"I suppose you're right, Avilyn," the King smiled, "I've done what I set out to do and I'm no worse for wear, so perhaps we should head back now."

"As his Majesty wishes," Captain Waxx cordially offered, "right dis way, Mon."

The two ships were resting in the secret cove.

It looked much different now that the chests full of plunder were removed.

It looked like a really great spot for fishing!

"Not just the treasure, Captain Waxx," the King announced, "this very cove belongs to The Scorpion now."

"Sire?" Waxx asked.

"This is The Scorpion's new home," he smiled, "The Scorpion's Den. I decree it."

CHAPTER FIVE

UNDER NEW MANAGEMENT

A full year went by with no sight or news of The Grand Ascendancy, and a lot has changed.

The King found a suitable bride, Brother Fost performed the ceremony and then decided to remain in Salvus Hus.

Halflings aren't normally found outside of their shires except on special occasions.

Fost had become weary of constant travel and battle and wanted to settle down in a place where we could easily find him.

Navari decided to remain on The Scorpion while Captain Rina and the crew of The Dragonfly resumed their self-chosen missions, checking in with us from time to time.

Nitch, however, wanted more adventure and decided, much to Balt's chagrin, the dwarven warrior was his new best friend.

The Scorpion's Den has become our chosen, collective home and has become a cozy, safe haven for the team and the crew, complete with a sizable cropping of wooden houses and a stable, all in the safety of the Hollow.

Due to the sudden, endless flow of money, The Scorpion was re-fitted with new heavy cannons, an updated walking mechanism, an armored hull, and brand-new dark sails.

Did I mention she has a new captain?

Captain Mario Waxx had failed to mention to any of us that he had a wife and two teenaged children living in the southern village of Bom'dabo.

Now that he was finally wealthy enough to retire comfortably, which was his plan from the beginning, he was retiring and going home.

"Bom'dabo?" I asked, "I lived so close to Bom'dabo for most of my life and never visited."

"Why would you?" Mario asked with a grin, "Dat's Drow territory."

The Drow elves are dark skinned, distant cousins to Seolfer elves, like Loher and me.

We never really got along.

I guess it's because Drow elves use dark magic while Seolfer elves use neutral magic.

We don't fight; we're not at war; we just don't see eye to eye when it comes to magic use.

Captain Waxx and the crew had taken the last year to train the team in the fundamentals of sailing and controlling a large sea vessel.

We've become fairly proficient and have taken The Scorpion out on our own under Waxx's supervision.

Waxx took particular care to teach Meeka, Kuchoff and me the really important parts about being the Captain and Senior Officers.

Loher had absolutely no interest in being an Officer, while Balt, Navari, and the pair of eline assassins decided it was best to be part of the newly formed, 'ground team.'

Anchored just off the shore near the village of Bom'dabo, the entire crew of The Scorpion, including my team, took a secret ballot vote to 'elect' The Scorpion's new captain.

Waxx counted the ballots and wrote the new captain's name on a slip of paper that he slipped into his pocket.

We stood on the deck in a large circle around Mario Waxx, Meeka Ashpin, Kuchoff Magnus and me.

"I, Captain Mario Waxx, captain of De Scorpion, hereby transfer ownership and command of De Scorpion and her crew to Captain..." he paused and looked around from face to face.

Everyone looked anxious and excited to hear the name of their new captain.

He cleared his throat and continued, "Captain Kuchoff Magnus."

The crew erupted in cheers and celebratory wishes.

"Choose yer First Mate, Mate," Balt yelled over the cheering.

The crew calmed down to hear the name.

Kuchoff smiled his famous toothy grin and announced, "Meeka Ashpin," he reached out to her and touched her hand, "Commander."

Meeka smiled and giggled in acceptance.

"That leaves you third in command," Loher cooed and kissed me.

"I'm fine with that," I replied, "I'm a ranger, not a sailor."

"Does that mean we're leaving the ship too?" Loher asked with concern in her voice.

"Not at all," I laughed, "like you, I didn't want to be in the top command. Third is simply fine with me."

———— ◆ ————

Bom'dabo was larger than I had imagined.

Thousands of huts were laid out in a grid-like pattern surrounding a single, large hut, larger than the rest.

This was the community center, education center and main shoppes.

Drow and human, a substantial portion, dark skinned like Mario Waxx, coexisted here in peace, with a diverse smattering of other good-ish creatures mixed in.

"Why don't we see more Drow in other towns?" Kuchoff asked.

"These are the first I've ever seen," Navari whispered.

"We're the first eline anyone alive has ever seen," Roash compared.

"Yes," I agreed, "but Drow are common dwellers here in this realm, and *it is* quite rare to see one."

"We rarely see outsiders as well," a Drow woman sang as she threw herself at Mario, "Welcome home, Baby!"

"We saw your ship drop anchor and *knew* you were home for a visit!" A young half human, half Drow elf girl squealed in excitement.

"Dat's not my ship," Mario smiled, "she's his," he said, thumbing the air at Captain Magnus.

Captain Magnus began to smile until he noticed an angry look suddenly wash over Mrs. Waxx's face.

"Mario Waxx," she pouted, "what have you done? Lost her in a bet??" She was fuming.

Mario stood straight and tall, fully expecting the incoming vulgar misunderstandings and patiently waited the storm out.

Calmly, he replied by dropped an exceptionally large diamond into her hand, "Deir's a whole lot more where dat came from."

"You're retiring?" she asked, her scowl turning into a smile.

"Ja Mon!" Waxx grinned.

"Thank you for bringing my husband home, Captain…"

"Magnus, Ma'am," Kuchoff smiled and shook her hand, "Kuchoff Magnus."

"Did you just say your name is Kuchoff?" A light skinned, middle aged human male asked from the street.

Out of the corner of his eye, Kuchoff could see Roash silently extend her natural claws.

"I did," Captain Magnus cautiously answered.

"I was just in Swapton two days ago and overheard a woman talking about you to a group of men and it doesn't sound good for you," the stranger reported.

"Come here, my friend," Captain Magnus prompted.

The man cautiously approached.

Captain Magnus reached into his pocket, produced a small gold coin, and handed it to the man, "You never saw me."

"Oh, look what I found on the path!" The man winked and moved along on his own business.

"With that my friend," Captain Magnus breathed, "we shall take our leave of you," he bowed low to Mario Waxx and his family.

"Go do sumtin' I couldn't do," Mario Waxx said as he grasped the new captain's hand in blessing, "An' try not ta sink 'er."

We all smiled and walked away from the former captain's home, "Is anyone interested in going to Larix?" I asked, "since we're so close."

The smile widened on Loher's face, and I noticed a slight perk in her step, "I wouldn't mind having a short visit," she said, "I've always wanted to see your house."

"We'd like to see it as well," Roash added excitedly.

Rion began to purr loud enough to attract attention from those around us.

"I'm going to go back to the ship and take her back to the Den," Captain Magnus announced, "we can't afford to have her sitting idle out in the open like that. Just send up a fireball or energy ball as a signal for us to come back," he smiled, "I'll have someone watching."

Meeka smiled at her adoptive son, now a man, now the captain of the famous Scorpion.

She was proud.

"I'm gonna go wit 'im," Balt chuckled, "ye 'magic types' go on ahead."

Nitch jumped from Balt's pack and landed on Rion's shoulder.

"*Nice jump!*" Roash complemented, impressed.

"Why me?" Rion growled.

"You're *dangerous!*" Nitch hissed into Rion's ear, making the eline purr again.

"All aboard that's coming aboard," Captain Magnus called as he struck out for The Scorpion.

Balt almost had to jog to keep up with the young man.

"He's going to make a fine captain," I smiled, "he's already choosing duty over adventure."

"I'm sure his duty *is* his adventure at this point," a small voice came muffled from somewhere in Rion's fur.

Rion was slightly wiggling around, purring in a jovial way as the errford nuzzled a nest in the eline's shoulder fur, "Comfy?" Rion sarcastically asked as the nuzzling finally stopped.

"Yes, thank you," the tiny, muffled voice replied.

Meeka giggled and playfully punched the assassin in the other shoulder.

Captain Magnus and Balt disappeared into the village as we turned toward the Seolfer Wudu and began to stroll down the path less traveled.

After a few hours of walking through the Seolfer Wudu, I began to recognize my surroundings, "Do you know where you are yet?" I asked my bride.

"No," she answered, looking around, "do you?"

"One of my uncles, on my mother's side, used to take me hunting here when I was a boy," I reminisced, "If you're still and quiet, the game will come to you."

"We should try it," Loher laughed and strung up her bow.

"I'm hungry," Rion purred and slunk down into the undergrowth, hiding himself perfectly.

Roash effortlessly jumped straight up into a tree and disappeared.

Navari, however, just backed up to a moss-covered tree and completely blended in.

I looked at Meeka as I reached for my hood, "Can you hide, or do you want to share my cloak?"

Meeka looked around at the forest around her and realized she stuck out like a candle in the dark, "Your cloak, if it's big enough," she decided.

I opened my cloak and Meeka crawled in close, Loher had done this with her once before, so I looked to her for instruction.

She was smiling and trying not to laugh as she shrugged her shoulders, pulled on her own hood, and disappeared.

I managed to cloak us well enough that if we held really still, we couldn't be seen.

Only a mere twenty minutes or so went by before we saw our first target.

A rabbit.

Loher steadied her breathing and took aim…

An arrow silently zipped through the air, finding purchase in the rabbit, killing it instantly.

"Nice shot!" I whispered.

"That wasn't my arrow," Loher whispered back.

"Whose...?" I began but noticed the rabbit had disappeared, "where'd it go?"

"I was watching the whole time and saw no one," Loher hissed in confusion.

"Shouldn't we be able to see an invisible person with these cloaks on?" Meeka asked.

"You're right," I agreed, "we should."

"Something's not right here," Loher stated, "there's another rabbit, let's see if it happens again."

We waited and watched and lo and behold, another arrow and another silent disappearing act.

Stunned and confused, we sat silently, watching two more rabbits disappear after being impaled by strange arrows.

A few moments after the killings had stopped and more rabbits and squirrels were frolicking around, we felt safe enough to decloak and move.

"No food?" Rion moaned.

"Oh," Loher laughed, "sorry."

She drew back her bowstring and let loose an arrow, finding purchase in a fat rabbit.

"Anyone else?" she asked.

We set up camp and decided to stay for the night.

Loher and I searched the area for any clues as to who or what had killed and taken the rabbits, but only discovered fresh large cat tracks unlike any I had ever seen.

"They're not eline," Roash confirmed, "so what other cat species can wield a bow?"

"None that I know of," I answered, "but I didn't know your species still existed before Errfordland."

"It shall remain a mystery," Loher sighed, "for now."

The next morning, we awoke to a beautiful sunrise and crisp autumn air.

Loher had already been out hunting and had brought back a mixed dozen fat rabbits and quails.

"I'm starting to miss Brother Fost," she sighed, "he would be the one to do all of this."

I got up and began to help her cook breakfast, "perhaps Cook should be on the ground team," I chuckled in jest.

Loher looked at me with a thoughtful gaze, smiled and returned to minding the fire, "It happened again," she stated and turned a rabbit on a spit.

"What do you mean?" Meeka asked as she too, began to help.

"The strange arrows and cat pawprints, the disappearing act," she said, "I went out cloaked and bagged a few bunnies, but then, I saw the quail."

"I like quail," Rion purred.

"So, I started following the quail, so I could nab a few at a time, when one of those strange arrows nearly hit me on its way to a rabbit near me, so I froze to observe." Loher blinked, "I didn't see who or what shot it and I couldn't hear a thing. Not even the arrow, but it disappeared all the same."

She took some meat off the fire and began to hand it out, "I looked around and only found those same cat tracks. Still warm."

"I may be able to track the cat," Navari spoke up, "I have thermal vision, when needed."

"You can see heat?" Nitch asked with a mouthful of quail.

"That is correct, my tiny friend," Navari giggled at the rarely seen and extremely cute creature.

"Why didn't you see it the first time?" Loher asked, "You were there."

"I didn't know to look for it," Navari defended, "and besides, I was standing too far away, I must be right up close to see them.

"Fair enough," Loher smiled and returned to her meal.

"Next time," Navari vowed.

We ate in silence, enjoying our meal until Rion let out a tremendous belch.

"Did you enjoy your food?" Meeka rhetorically giggled.

"I have to admit, Loher," I laughed, "your cooking far exceeds Brother Fost's, and you can tell him I said that."

"Agreed," Roash cheered, raising her mug.

Loher blushed, "You're biased," she said, "I'm your wife; you have to say nice stuff like that."

"You're not *my* wife," Roash laughed, "and I'm not nice."

Rion, with an exaggerated worried look on his face, nodded vigorously in agreement, almost shaking poor Nitch from his furry perch.

"We should get going," I said as I got up and stretched, "before we waste this beautiful day."

We struggled to get the camp packed up in an orderly fashion, and quickly realized that Brother Fost did well more than any of us gave him credit for.

I could see it on Loher and Meeka's faces, we all missed him.

We continued on the only trail leading in the direction of Larix, and I vaguely recognized where I was, but the fork in the path we had just arrived at had me confused.

My uncle always led the way, and I was just a young child at the time he had taken me this way, so I was confused on which way to go.

"Are we lost?" Meeka teased, not knowing the situation.

"Yes," I breathed in confusion, "I'm unsure on which way to go."

"I was joking," the wizard replied, "but, okay."

Both paths were equally as untraveled as the path we were currently on, so the obvious was off the table.

"Do we want to split up and go both directions and return here after a few minutes, or just pick a path and hope for the best?" I asked.

"How dangerous is it here?" Meeka asked.

Rion snorted.

"This is our homeland," Loher stated, "you're safer here than you would be on the path to Salvus Hus."

"Really?"

"Mmm, hmm."

"What about our unseen friend?" Nitch countered.

"What are *you* afraid of?" Roash laughed in contempt, "you're virtually immortal *and* you're riding on the toughest eline I've ever known," she bragged, "and I know them all."

"I was only stating a fact," Nitch calmly replied, and gently stroked Rion's shoulder fur.

"I don't think we have to worry about our unseen friend," Loher explained, "if it wanted us dead," she paused, "we would be dead by now."

"Good point," we all agreed as if rehearsed.

"I'm still curious about it though," Navari added.

"As am I," Loher agreed.

"Which way?" I asked, bringing the focus back to our problem at hand.

"I think we should split up and meet back here in an hour," Meeka suggested, "Loher, Roash and I will go this way and the rest of you, that way."

"Aye, Commander," I happily conceded and led Navari, Rion, and Nitch down our assigned path.

It wasn't long before I began to recognize my surroundings and I was sure I had taken the correct path.

"Loher! Meeka!" I called out...

No answer.

Rion chuckled.

I tried whistling.

No answer.

Rion chuckled again and puffed out his chest.

"They must be too far away to hear me," I groaned.

Rion suddenly let out a deafening roar that was answered immediately with a distant roar.

Rion roared again and sat down, waiting.

"Why yell or whistle when you can roar?" I asked myself and leaned against a tree.

Navari sat near me and began to hum a melodic tune.

After a moment, birds began to chime in, or at least it sounded like it to me.

The sound of her humming was ever so relaxing and after a while, Rion was purring loud enough for me to hear.

"My words to Onh, Rion," Roash laughed as her half of the team arrived, "I could hear you purring from a good distance away."

"She was humming," Rion purred.

"I hum to relax," the medusan stated, "it lulls others to sleep if I wish it so."

"Is that a trait of your race?" I asked.

"I'm unsure," Navari answered, "I don't know much about my people. I was sold into slavery as a child, but escaped, thought to be dead."

"I'm so sorry to hear that," Meeka soothed, "but so happy you escaped and are with us now."

I assumed that Navari smiled under her hood, but I couldn't be sure.

I cleared my throat and pointed down the path, "I recognize this path," I stated and began to lead the way.

The team followed, and after less than an hour's travel, we arrived at the gates of Larix.

⋅⋅⋅◆⋅⋅⋅

I stopped before entering, "Loher, you claim to be the best thief in the realm, right?"

She blushed, "I, uh... never said *the best*..."

"Fair enough," I slyly smiled, "but if I may quote you from when we first met," I cleared my throat, "Quote: 'there has been no lock so far that I have not been able to pick and no trap set so far that I have not been able to disarm or get around. There is also nothing that is not affixed to a stable surface that I cannot steal.' End quote.

"So," she blinked, impressed that I remembered every word, but refused to show it, "what about it?"

"As a team," I began, "I want you to sneak in, find my house and steal the dagger. I'll silently observe."

"Which dagger?" Rion asked.

"As far as I know," I scratched my head in thought, "there is only one dagger I left behind."

My companions looked at each other, wondering if they should rise to the challenge, or tell me to get my own damn dagger.

"What are we waiting for?" A muffled voice came from virtually nowhere.

Rion began to dig into his shoulder fur.

"You really should get that checked out, my friend," Navari quipped, "looks to me like you've got critters."

"And you have snakes for hair," Nitch teased back, now free from the fur.

Navari giggled under her hood.

"Too easy," Loher laughed and put up her hood, "for me."

I too, put up my own hood so I could still see where she was and what she was doing.

I kept in contact with Navari and the eline assassins by whispering.

"Usually, on assassinations," Roash began, talking to the air next to me, "we begin with a little intel."

"We never go in blind," Rion added.

"Alright," I compromised, "My house is near the orchard, that's all I can tell you."

Immediately, I lost sight of all four of my contestants.

I decided to take the scenic route to my house, with my hood up so I could see Loher, (if I could find her again,) *and* so the others couldn't see me.

I made it to my house around five minutes later and the five of them were already standing there, visible, waiting on me.

Navari had the dagger in her hand.

I walked up to them and removed my hood.

"First off," I raised a finger in the air, "how did you know this was my house?"

"I could still smell your feet from a hundred meters away," Loher said with a loving smile.

The others just smiled and nodded in agreement.

"They're *that* bad?" I asked.

"What are *you* doing back around here, Half-breed?" A gruff voice called out from behind me.

I spun around to see a group of more than a dozen elves, armed with bows, standing just off my property line.

Both Roash and Rion unsheathed their natural claws.

Rion began to purr.

"Friends of yours?" Navari asked, lightly fingering the edge of her hood.

"I know a few of them," Loher whispered, "they're good people. For them to act this way toward you only means you did something wrong."

"Now it makes sense why you wanted us to sneak here," Roash growled.

I raised my hands in the air and slowly began to walk toward the elves.

"Thunor," Loher gasped, her fingertips hovering over her bottom lip.

I turned and smiled back at her.

I continued to walk toward the group of elves, and when I got close enough, the leader lunged at me and embraced me in a warm, inviting hug.

"There was a short time I thought you dead," he said as he held me at arm's length and looked at me up and down with affection.

He waved the rest of the elves off, to continue their hunting trip.

"No," I laughed, "just married."

"Ugh!" He groaned, "Even **worse,**" he chortled, "which is the un-lucky bride, so I can put her out of her misery?"

"Touch her and die," Rion growled and stepped in front of Loher.

Rion towered over the elf and extended the claws of his right paw-hand.

"Rion," I began, trying to calm him, "this is my friend, Jarrus," I explained, "he was only joking."

Rion began to chuckle, "So am I," he purred and stepped aside.

"I was beginning to wish I hadn't sent the hunting party away so soon," Jarrus gulped and wiped sweat from his brow.

"One good turn," Rion laughed, "deserves another."

"I don't quite understand, my friend, say..." Jarrus looked at Rion and Roash, "what are you?"

"Eline," Roash answered.

"You don't say..." Jarrus breathed and visually inspected the pair, "You're not supposed to exist, yet here you are."

"Ta-da..." Rion purred.

"Well," I said and put my hand on his shoulder, gently guiding him in the direction his hunting party went, "your party shouldn't be too far if you hurry. We have a ship to catch, so if you would be so kind..."

Confused and still in awe of the eline, "I. Yeah, yeah, sure," he stammered and began to leave, "are you going to be around...?"

"Ship," Meeka echoed.

"Oh, right," Jarrus laughed, "good morrow," he called back and set off running.

"Leaving?" Loher softly chuckled when Jarrus was out of earshot, "So soon?"

"What was *that* all about?" Roash wondered aloud.

"Oh, just an old, annoying friend I had hoped *not* to run into," I answered and spotted my dagger in Navari's hand, "you took the dagger?" I asked the medusan healer.

She handed me the dagger, "I was the only one that could," she answered, "Rion couldn't fit through the window, Roash and Meeka decided not to brave the foot stench, so I slipped in and found the dagger straight away."

"I unlocked the window," Loher added, pretending to pout.

"Loher unlocked the window," Navari, agreed with a tiny giggle forming in her voice.

I inspected the crystal dagger I had owned since I was a small boy.

Memories of creating it with my father filled my head.

He even taught me how to use it, fight with it, and most importantly, take care of it.

It was really the only thing I had left to remember him by, so I carefully placed it in my bag and looked at my team.

"Where's your house?" I asked Loher.

"Right here," she smiled and pointed at my house.

"I mean, where did you live before?" I laughed.

The smile disappeared from her face, "I have no business there," she stated and began to stroll toward the road.

Meeka shot me a look as if to say, 'don't ask right now,' so I put my arm around Loher's shoulder and just silently pulled her closer and continued strolling.

It was getting late, so we decided to spend the night at my house.

A good thing too, as it began to storm.

My thoughts went out to Jarrus and his poor hunting party, out in a storm like this.

It was his foolish idea to go hunting in the first place.

"What are you thinking about?" Loher asked as she handed me a bowl of soup.

Lightning lit up the sky, followed closely by a round of rolling thunder that shook the walls.

Dust lightly sprinkled down from the rafters.

"That fool, Jarrus," I chuckled softly, "leading his team into a storm like this."

A soft flickering glow from the fireplace lit her face in such a way that she seemed to dance to a silent tune.

Another round of lightning bolts brightly lit the windows and enhanced the illusion.

A string of deafening thunder cracks split the night air.

Meeka began to giggle.

"Is everything okay, Meeka?" Roash asked, out of curiosity, not concern.

Meeka looked up and smiled, "Thunderstorms remind me of when I was just a girl, learning magic from the great wizard, Ficolus."

"Atop Exland Mountain," I added.

"Exland?" Navari questioned, "Isn't that where Lemac said Amaliya was projecting herself from? The top of Exland Mountain?"

Lightning continued to flash and flicker in the night sky and a chorus of rolling thunder booms kept along in time.

"You're right," Meeka concurred and snapped her fingers, "that should have occurred to me the moment he said it."

"It's okay," I stated, "Commander," I added to remind her, and everyone else, that she was dealing with a lot when this all took place.

Meeka smiled and nodded her head at me in appreciation.

Off in the corner, nearest to the fireplace, Rion and Roash were asleep and purring lightly, Nitch snuggled deeply into Rion's fur.

I could see that Loher was feeling drowsy, and she immediately confirmed my suspicions by stating, "I'm going to sleep tonight."

"No reverie?" I rhetorically asked with a grin.

She smiled, excused herself and retired to the bed.

Meeka began to quietly giggle again, "Navari is asleep as well," she said, nodding her head in the direction of the mysterious healer, stretched out in front of the fire.

I could ever so slightly hear her breathing deeply.

"Take the bed," I offered the wizard.

"Are you sure?" she asked.

I smiled and waved her off to the bed, "Go, before I change my mind," I teased.

She smiled sweetly and crawled in next to Loher.

By the time I removed my boots and settled into a chair, Meeka was snoring, or 'purring' as she likes to say.

The thunderstorm continued through the night and finally let up in the wee hours of the morning.

I was enjoying watching over my family as they slept.

It really didn't matter to me why Loher didn't want to go to her former home.

She *was* home, here with me and our new family.

I barely slept, but still felt rested and refreshed.

⸺◆⸺

We had a quick breakfast of some porridge I had in my cupboard; the eline pair went hunting and came back satisfied.

"I kind of missed the rocking of the sea last night," Meeka yawned between spoonfuls of porridge.

"I didn't miss your snoring," Loher teased and lightly elbowed the wizard in her ribs.

Nitch strolled across the table with a half hopping motion and approached my bowl, "May I?" the Errford politely asked.

"Be my guest," I smiled and gently nudged my bowl toward him.

He perched on the edge of my bowl and tried a bit.

He must have decided that he liked it because he immediately began to pick out chunks and devour them whole.

"Slow down, little friend," Rion chuckled, "you're going to get sick."

"Chew," Meeka suggested.

The Errford looked up and smiled, porridge dripping from his whiskers, nodded, and slowly continued to gorge himself.

"I'm glad it's not *my* fur..." Roash commented to the room.

Rion groaned and slumped onto the bed.

***

We snuck back out of town, in case Jarrus decided to pay another visit, and didn't allow ourselves to be seen until we were well out of view.

"It's a two day walk back to Bom'dabo," I casually mentioned as we began further down the path.

"And probably another half day until The Scorpion arrives to pick us up," Meeka added.

"Perhaps on the way, we will uncover the mystery of the disappearing rabbits?" Loher jested.

Roash and Navari agreed with that sentiment.

The autumn air was becoming chilly and the leaves on the trees were beginning to fall.

Our footfalls made a satisfying crunch with every step.

We walked for what seemed like hours, talking amongst ourselves, telling stories, and singing songs.

Nitch even decided to periodically dismount his eline steed and scramble around in the trees and fallen leaves.

It was at such a moment, when a large, tan colored cat with black tufts on the tips of its large ears, pounced on the poor errford and began to play with him.

It happened so quickly, Nitch had no time to react, until he got away for a moment.

His blue protection orb suddenly surrounded him, and the cat was just harmlessly playing with a ball at that point.

As this was happening, we all had drawn our weapons and were about to strike when we heard a whistle and then a voice, "Euka, los dit!" the disembodied voice screamed.

The cat immediately discontinued its behavior, stopped the ball's motion with its paw, then sat quietly as a Drow elf emerged from the brush.

Not much younger than Kuchoff, she stood before us, wearing a cloak that looked as if it were made from actual shadows sewn together over forest toned leather armor.

She was hard to see, even in the open as close as she was to us.

In her left hand, she was carrying a bow that looked similar to Loher's, and in her right, a quiver of those strange arrows.

"Cat prints explained," I eased and lowered my bow.

Loher lowered hers as well, "Strange arrows, explained," she nodded.

Navari took her hands away from her hood and looked as if she relaxed a little.

"Kom hier," the Drow commanded.

The cat got up and walked to her and laid at her feet.

Nitch immediately dove into Rion's shoulder and began to bark at the cat.

"Allow me to apologize for Euka," the Drow spoke in the common tongue, "she loves to play with squirrels."

"Ek is geen eekhoring nie," Nitch countered, "ek is 'n errford."

Our new encounter looked surprised and shocked at her new knowledge, "It speaks!"

Nitch laughed nervously, "Of course I do, like I said, I'm no squirrel, I'm an errford. My name is Nitch."

Euka slyly got up and began to investigate us, beginning with me.

"My name is Lybiidae," she bowed, "and this is Euka, my caracal companion."

We each briefly introduced ourselves as Euka showed herself off proudly.

Euka was about 123 cm (4 foot) long from the tip of her nose to the tip of her tail, 42 cm (a foot and a half) tall from her paw pads to her shoulder and weighed approximately 45kg (100 lb.)

"She's gorgeous," Meeka squeaked, "so are you, but just look at *her*!" She stooped lower when Euka began to sniff her and got a semi decent hug before the caracal moved on to Roash.

'This ought to be interesting,' I thought to myself as one 'cat' sniffed the other.

She took her time sniffing the eline assassins and seemed to enjoy being near them, because she began to rub against their legs, circling around and going in for another rub.

After a moment, she laid down between the two and began to purr.

"I think she likes us," Rion laughed.

Roash began to stroke Euka's fur.

"Staan op," Lybiidae requested of her companion, "ons gaan."

Euka didn't move.

"Staan op," she repeated.

Euka reluctantly stood up and sauntered toward her companion.

"We're on our way to Bom'dabo," I mentioned to see if I got any reaction from her.

No reaction.

"You're welcome to join us," I continued.

Lybiidae simply pulled her hood over her head and virtually disappeared into the woods, followed closely by Euka, who stopped, looked back at us, and then disappeared.

"Did anyone else notice that her feet never made a sound?" Loher asked as she purposely stepped on a twig and made it snap.

"No," Meeka sighed, "I was too enamored of her *caracal.*"

"I noticed," Navari replied and caught up to Loher, "I've seen boots like that before. They leave no prints of any kind, or ripples in water, as well as making the wearer silent when walking."

"Boots of Calm," Meeka informed from behind, "and she is wearing a Shadow Cloak."

"Her bow looked like it was made by the same hands that made mine," Loher said, holding up her bow, "and her arrows were the same as our unseen friend's arrows."

"She seemed disinterested in us," I commented and stepped over a large rock that had been there as long as I could remember.

"Her caracal sure seemed interested in *us,*" Roash laughed and motioned to Rion and herself.

Nitch moaned and hid in Rion's fur.

"Euka's ears reminded me of Reetah's," Rion purred and almost tripped over that same rock.

"Only smaller," Roash laughed, and Rion joined in.

"Who is Reetah?" Meeka asked with a toothy grin.

"My sister," Rion answered.

"Where is she?"

"Errfordland," Rion answered.

"Why didn't she come with you?" Meeka drilled, becoming slightly annoying.

"Because her mate is a useless clod," Roash cut in, "He's worthless and so is she for staying with him."

"Wow," Meeka giggled, "tell us how you really feel, sister."

"She was also my best friend," Roash calmly completed.

We walked on in broken silence for the next few hours until we arrived at our previous camping spot.

"I could use a rest," Meeka announced, "anyone else?"

We all stopped and set down our gear, relieved to be stopping for the night.

"I'm hungry," Rion growled.

"When are you *not* hungry?" Nitch giggled.

"I'll eat you," Rion teased.

"You'll only die trying," the errford playfully countered.

"Is that true, Nitch?" I asked as I began to start a campfire.

"Did you see any large predators on the island?" Nitch asked.

"No," I answered after a moment's thought, "other than the eline."

"They all died off from either lack of food or trying to eat us," Nitch smiled, "we have no natural enemies...anymore."

"So, Euka would have died if she tried to eat you instead of just playing with you?" Meeka asked, becoming horrified at the thought.

"Without a doubt," Nitch yawned and closed his eyes, snuggled into Rion's shoulder.

⸻◆⸻

We awoke to a stoked fire, fish, and quail cooking over the fire and three sleeping 'cats.'

Lybiidae was in the middle of cleaning a few fat rabbits, humming as she worked.

Loher was taking the time to fletch a mess of arrows.

"Well, good morning, stranger," I yawned as I got up.

Lybiidae nodded at me and continued her work.

I looked over at Loher and shrugged.

"Apparently," Loher began with a smile, "Euka decided that she wanted to be part of *this* pride and wouldn't let Lybiidae get very far from us."

Lybiidae shyly smiled as if to ask if it was okay.

"How are you with sea travel?" I asked the Drow.

"Fairly used to it," she answered, "although it has been a while."

"And dwarves?" Rion asked as he cuddled Euka.

"I'm fine with dwarves, but if you say you have orc or hobgoblin friends," she scowled, "We're going to have to break Euka's heart and stay here."

"Quite the contrary," Navari added, "our team and crew are, sort of, at war with them.

Lybiidae suddenly began to smile, "Count me in," she said with a balled-up fist.

"Captain Magnus will be pleased," Meeka smiled.

"I've never heard of him," Lybiidae commented, "which ship?"

"The Scorpion," Meeka proudly answered.

"But that's Mario Waxx's ship," she said with worry on her face, "is he dead?"

"No," I answered, "retired, and with great fortune."

Lybiidae slowly closed her eyes in relief, smiled and sighed a big sigh.

"Have you ever been on The Scorpion?" I asked out of curiosity.

"Once," she answered, "when I was very young."

We sat and ate, getting to know each other a little better.

Euka seemed to bounce between the eline and the Drow, enjoying the attention she was receiving.

A few moments after breakfast was gone and the cooking gear was washed and put away, I announced, "It's another day's travel to Bom'dabo," I said and began to pack up my gear, "we should be going."

Lybiidae began to howl out in laughter, "A *day?*" she chortled, "I can get us there in three hours."

"Impossible without mounts," I argued, taken aback by her laughter.

"I didn't mean to laugh so hard," she sort of apologized, "I forget that the Seolfer don't know the Drow's tricks."

"Tricks?" Meeka asked.

"Follow me," Lybiidae suggested and grabbed up her gear.

Euka was immediately at her heels.

We all followed suit as soon as the fire was extinguished and followed the Drow into the woods.

She led us down a rarely used, hidden path that went on for about fifteen minutes until we arrived at a hollow tree.

"Seolfer," she giggled and disappeared into the tree.

Euka followed her in.

We looked at each other for a second and then bravely followed the strange companions in.

Inside the hollow tree, the ground sloped sharply down and then leveled out a few meters down.

Lybiidae and Euka were waiting at the bottom.

"I can't see a thing!" Meeka complained and cast a light spell.

The area lit up like daylight, revealing a tunnel wide and tall enough to ride a horse in.

"Okay," I admitted, "you win, Lybiidae."

"Three hours," she smiled, "straight on through."

We began walking in the eerie silence of being underground.

No wind.

No bird songs.

Nothing except for footsteps and the sound of your own blood rushing through the veins in your ears.

If anyone spoke, their voice would echo through the tunnel and become painful to the ears, so we didn't talk much.

The air was dank and damp.

It smelled like rotting leaves and putrid mud.

The hours seemed to stretch on for days because we had no sun to tell time by, and just when I was about to ask how much further, I saw a bit of natural light ahead of us and began to smell the salty sea air.

Mere moments later, we emerged from the base of another hollow tree at the closest edge of town.

We had made it to Bom'dabo roughly three hours later, according to the sun.

"Amazing," I admitted.

The Drow elf smiled.

We strolled through the town, taking in the history and the sights, and when we reached the shoreline, Meeka sent up a large fireball into the sky.

"What was *that* for?" Lybiidae asked, watching it arc through the air and disappear into the sea.

"A signal for The Scorpion to come pick us up," Meeka answered.

We sat on the beach, watching Rion, Roash and Euka play in the sand.

After a while, Lybiidae turned to Nitch and said, "I think this will be good for Euka."

Nitch smiled and munched on a random nut he had picked up on the trail, "Do you think it would be alright if I were to ride on Euka's back once in a while?"

"If she'll let you," Lybiidae guessed.

"You won't mind?" the errford asked with bright eyes.

"No weight on *my* back," she replied.

The errford smiled and took another giant munch from his treat.

"You're not afraid of her?" Lybiidae asked, a bit surprised.

Nitch shook his head and swallowed the mouthful he was chewing on, "I don't mean to boast, but I'm virtually immortal."

"Virtually?" she asked.

"I can die from illness and old age," he explained, "but weapons and magic have no effect on my kind."

"Even *dark* magic?" she asked.

"Won't work," he said, "not on me."

"Interesting," she breathed, stroking her chin in thought, "how does one acquire these abilities?"

"Simple!" Nitch squeaked, "keep an errford with you in battle and we will keep you safe."

"There are more of you on the ship?" she asked.

"Unfortunately, no," he said with a frown, "it's just me."

"Who decides who gets you in battle?" she asked.

"I do," he said, "I choose who I go with and if I even go."

"Good," Lybiidae smiled, "I was worried for a moment that you had no choice."

"These are good people," Nitch vouched, "you'll see."

The Scorpion was arriving near the shore.

"How do you choose who you go with?" Lybiidae asked as he hopped onto her shoulder, and they began to walk to the ship.

Nitch laughed, "You're going to think I'm insane," Nitch warned, "but I go with whoever is going to be in the most danger."

"That makes the most sense," Lybiidae concurred, "why waste your skills or talents on a fight not worth fighting?"

"Not exactly," Nitch countered.

"What then?"

"Why waste your skills or talents on a boring fight?"

"I think I'm beginning to like you, Nitch."

"All aboard that's coming aboard," a sailor yelled from the dinghy sent out to retrieve us.

Somehow, we all fit on the small dinghy and made it safely back aboard The Scorpion.

"Permission to come aboard, Captain?" Meeka requested.

"Granted, Commander and team," Captain Magnus smiled, "who and what do we have here?" he curiously asked as he set eyes on Lybiidae and Euka.

"Aren't you a little young to be a ship's captain?" Lybiidae asked and offered her hand.

"I'm older than you, I'll bet," he countered and helped her aboard.

"I'm not a ship's captain," Lybiidae countered back.

"Who *are* you?" Captain Magnus asked as Euka effortlessly jumped aboard.

"I am called Lybiidae N'Jinga, and this is Euka."

"Captain Kuchoff Magnus, at your service, Ma'am."

Chapter Six

EXLAND

We were out to sea, showing Lybiidae parts of the realm she never thought she would ever get to see, while also trying to taunt the Grand Ascendancy into showing themselves.

Days passed with no sign of them.

"I think we should go explore Exland Mountain," Meeka suggested, "perhaps my old teacher, Ficolus is still alive and has a few answers."

"Good Idea, Mom, err... Commander," Captain Magnus smiled, "take us to Exland," he informed the helm.

"Aye," the helm replied, "Exland in two hours, Captain."

"I'll go an' assemble t'e ground team," Balt sang as he jogged away from the bridge.

"I admire his adventurous spirit," Captain Magnus commented as he and Meeka began to walk to the hold.

"You have the bridge," Meeka informed the helmsman as she exited the bridge.

Aye, Ma'am," the helmsman acknowledged.

We all assembled in the hold outside of our cabins.

"We're headed to Exland Mountain," Captain Magnus announced, "we'll be there in less than two hours. I need three volunteers to go with us and search for answers as to Amaliya's whereabouts."

Without even having to mention it, Balt was the first to step forward, followed closely by Rion.

Nitch was bouncing on the deck between the pair of warriors.

"Roash," Captain Magnus asked in confusion, "you're not going?"

"I will, if no one else wants a chance to go," she purred.

"Perhaps I should go," Navari hissed, "I have the skeleton key to locked lips."

"Then it's settled," Captain Magnus agreed, "grab your gear and report to the bridge in ninety minutes."

The team disassembled and began to gather their gear.

"If ya need any weapons 'r armor fixed," Balt called out, "give 'em over."

"We haven't battled since you fixed them last," Rion moaned and showed the dwarf the blade of his short sword.

"Ah, guid," the dwarf smiled, "let's go git some eats."

Rion began to purr in agreement.

"Ye comin' wit' us?" Balt asked Navari.

"No, thank you," she replied as she inspected every centimeter of her whip.

"Suit yourself," Rion purred as the two warriors headed for the mess hall.

Exland Mountain loomed large as we approached it.

I decided to remain aboard The Scorpion as a team of my companions, led by Captain Magnus, explored the mystical mountain.

From all I could gather from stories and conversations, this is what happened...

Instead of using a dinghy, Meeka blinked the team to shore.

The rocky terrain was barren of any type of plant or animal life as if it had all been wiped away, clean.

"Stick together until we know what we're dealing with," Captain Magnus announced.

"I suggest we circle around the base of the island and work our way up," Meeka stated.

"Agreed," Captain Magnus smiled and began to walk the shoreline.

The team walked for hours, looking for any clue, but finding nothing.

"Perhaps we should split up into teams," Navari suggested, "we'll cover more ground that way."

"I agree," Meeka breathed.

"So do I," Captain Magnus began, "I was trying to figure out how to split the team and decided to have Nitch split the team."

"Why me?" Nitch asked.

"Why not?" Captain Magnus countered, "You're just as much a part of the crew as anyone else."

Nitch jumped down from Captain Magnus's shoulder and looked at the team, "Meeka, Balt and Navari on one team," he decided, "that way Meeka can blink to us if they find anything, and if *we* find anything, Rion can roar."

"Will that work?" Captain Magnus asked, a bit skeptical.

The entire team expressed their agreement in a jumble of yeses with great enthusiasm.

Convinced, Captain Magnus agreed, and the two teams set out searching.

Three quarters of the way up the mountain, after six hours of searching, just as the sun was about to set, Rion let out a deafening roar that seemed to echo throughout the Haze cove.

"That was *loud*," Meeka giggled as she and her team appeared from out of a puff of pink smoke.

"That was quick, where were you?" Nitch asked, perched alone on a rock.

"Just around that bend and down a way." Meeka pointed.

"What did you find?" Navari asked.

"Rion and Captain Magnus are eager to go in," Nitch advised, motioning to an unnatural entrance into the mountain.

"It's too dark to see very far in," Captain Magnus grinned.

"We need magic," Rion stated, "or a torch."

"Couldn't *you* cast a light spell?" Meeka asked Captain Magnus.

"I'm conserving my energy," Kuchoff replied, "in case Amaliya is in there."

"Very good idea," Meeka agreed and patted her adoptive son on the back.

The entrance lit up as Meeka cast a simple light spell.

The passage seemed to go in for quite a long distance until darkness took over.

"After you, Master Dwarf," Kuchoff invited Balt to lead the way.

"Now yer talkin'," Balt grinned as he gripped his Great Axe and entered the tunnel.

"Rion, would you mind protecting the rear?" Kuchoff asked.

"Nitch?" Rion purred.

Nitch scrambled up Rion's leg and settled into his shoulder nest.

"T'e enemy ain't gonna kill t'emselves," Balt roared and began down the long, dark tunnel.

Rion roared after him.

"If anyone *is* in here," Navari laughed, "they know we're coming."

The tunnel ran straight forward for around an hour's worth of walking and ended with a pristine circular staircase carved with great skill into the innards of the mountain, leading up.

Mmm...Inviting," Balt quipped as he approached the stairs.

"Have you ever been here, Meeka?" Kuchoff asked as the team stood at the bottom of the staircase.

"If I have," she tried to remember, "I don't remember it, but I was just a young, excited girl at the time. One of several other students."

"This is a school?" Rion asked.

"Of sorts," Meeka answered, "for magic."

"Cirdan should come here," Rion laughed and after thinking about it, Meeka and Kuchoff began to laugh as well.

"I don't git it," Balt spat in confusion, making Kuchoff laugh even harder.

After the laughter subsided, Meeka wiped tears from her eyes and cheeks, then cleared her throat, "Shall we?" she asked as she motioned up the stairs.

It was just a moment's climb up until they were blocked by a locked door.

"Does anyone have any lockpicks?" Captain Magnus asked, examining the lock, wishing Loher had come with them.

No one had any.

Navari tried to pick the lock with a dagger to no avail.

Rion tried using brute force, but only succeeded bruising his shoulder and knocking a small piece of the door loose.

Balt attempted to chop at the door with his Great Axe and only opened a small crack in the bottom.

"I can fit through that," Nitch squeaked in excitement, "I'll go through and see if I can unlock the door or find the key."

"I like that," Captain Magnus eagerly agreed.

Nitch peeked through the hole in the door and instantly brought his head back, "I don't think it will be necessary," he whispered, "we've attracted some attention."

The sound of a key sliding into the lock from the other side could be heard.

CLICK.

The door was unlocked.

The team took a few steps back away from the door as it slowly began to open, ready to defend themselves.

Balt gripped his Great Axe and began to softly growl, a smile stretching from ear to ear.

Soon after, Rion began growling, claws of his left paw-hand extended, short sword in his right.

Navari stood in the shadows and fingered the edge of her hood, while Meeka began charging up a round of energy balls and Captain Magnus drew his katana.

Nitch involuntarily became surrounded with a light blue glow.

The door swung open, revealing a frail old man dressed in grey wizard's robes, "I thought I heard a knock," the old man wheezed and stepped aside, "come in, come in," he beckoned and coughed.

"Why does t'is always 'appen?" Balt complained and kicked a chunk of the door down the stairs.

"What's wrong, Balt?" Navari asked.

"I git all worked up fer a fight," the dwarven warrior grumbled, "an' it turns out ta be an ol' man 'r sumptin' like t'at."

"That's good, isn't it?" she asked.

"Na fer me," he sulked, "we went t'rough t'at whole damn Hollow again, an' na one damn olyame."

"I'm sorry, Balt," she soothed.

"An' I didn't even git ta kill Monty again."

Navari led the pouting dwarf through the doorway and closed it behind her.

"Ahh, Meeka Ashpin," the old wizard cackled as he offered everyone a seat in his parlor, "you know, you're the very first student I've ever had that has come back for a visit?"

"Ever, Master Ficolus?" Meeka asked in surprise.

"Ever," he coughed, "after one hundred and ..." he thought for a moment and added, "**Two** hundred and six years of teaching."

"Impossible, for a human," Rion sighed.

"I know of your ancestors, eline." The old wizard glared at the giant cat.

"I'm sure he meant no offence, Master," Meeka stepped in.

"I'm sure not," Ficolus agreed, "I'm sorry, but in my day, eline folks didn't talk." He explained, "But I'm sure you were never aware of that."

"No, Master," Rion agreed, "May I call you, 'Master'?"

"It's who I am," the wizard cackled and wheezed, "now then," he said and stared at Navari, "let's see what you're hiding under your hood."

"I dare not, Master," Navari hissed.

"You're a medusan, aren't you?" Ficolus guessed.

"I am," she answered, "and half human."

"And you inherited your medusan traits?"

"Some," she admitted, "not all."

"Can you control them?" he asked.

"Well enough," she said, nervously.

"Then take off your hood and control them," he cackled, "I'd very much like to see your face."

She looked around nervously, "What about the others?" she asked with obvious fear in her voice.

"Are they not your friends?" he asked, "Your family?"

"We are," Meeka urged, "I want to see your face too."

"So do I," Captain Magnus chimed in.

"I already have," Nitch said, "and I'm still alive."

"You're immortal," Rion laughed.

"Virtually," Nitch countered with a raised pointer finger.

"Balt," Meeka coaxed, "say something."

"WOT?" Balt growled, "I donna care wot she looks like, as long as we get on well wit' each ot'er."

"Do we Balt?" Navari asked as she fingered the edge of her hood, "do we get along well?"

"Aye, Lass," Balt uttered, "we git on just foine."

"Would you like to see my face, Balt?" she asked.

"I've *been* curious," he admitted.

Navari stood there; her fingertips closed around the edges of her hood.

She took a deep breath, closed her eyes, and removed her hood.

"Well," Balt stated as a matter of a fact, "yer na as ugly as I guessed ye'd be."

"BALT!" Meeka snapped.

"WOT?"

Snakes danced around on Navari's scalp where only hair would normally be.

Her face seemed distorted by the firelight and the shadows from the writhing snakes; also, because she was squeezing her eyes shut tight, puffing out her cheeks and wrinkling the corners of her eyes.

"It's okay, Meeka," Navari soothed, "I've learned to accept Balt's rudeness as absolute candor."

"Absolute candor," Balt repeated, "I like t'at."

"Balt," Navari continued, her eyes squeezed tight, "I value your opinion because I *know* it's the truth."

"Open your eyes," Ficolus urged.

Navari turned toward the sound of his voice, stood still and silent for a moment and then slowly cracked open her eyelids.

Slowly, at first, but gradually faster until her eyes were fully open.

She looked human, besides a slight hunch-like curve in her back, an extra-long neck, powerful looking jaws, and the obvious snakes in her brown and black hair.

"Do you feel better?" the old wizard asked.

"I'm scared, Master," Navari whispered.

"Of what, my child?"

"Turning you all into stone, or worse," she shivered.

"Is that what you *want* to do?" the old man asked.

"No!" Her answer was immediate.

"Then," Ficolus cackled, "don't turn us all to stone."

"Or worse," Rion chuckled.

Nitch giggled and jumped from Rion's shoulder to the old man's shoulder and then to Navari's shoulder and settled into her hood.

"I guess I won't be using my hood for a while," Navari chuckled and began to relax.

"Oh, where are my manners," Ficolus sputtered with a cough, "may I offer anyone some tea?"

"Actually, Master," Meeka gained his attention, "we were wondering if you knew anything about the Grand Ascendancy."

Ficolus' face suddenly showed recognition and fear.

"Do ye 'ave anyt'ing stronger t'an tea?" Balt quipped.

"The Grand Ascendancy," Ficolus repeated in faux thought as he produced a fat jug and handed it to the dwarf with an obvious wink.

Balt eagerly snatched up the jug, pulled the cork and sniffed it, "Ooh hoo *hoo!*" Balt coughed with excitement and took a swig, "Ahhh... T'at's t'e stuff," he took another tiny swig and offered it to Rion.

Rion took a sniff and sneezed, refusing the jug.

"More fer me," Balt laughed and took another swig, "Cap'n?"

"No, thank you, Balt," Captain Magnus refused as well.

The dwarf silently offered the jug around the room, and other than the old wizard himself, everyone else refused.

"How about Amaliya Magnus?" Captain Magnus asked, trying to contain his curiosity, "Do you know of her?"

"She was one of my students," Ficolus remembered, "in the class just before yours, Meeka."

"Was she any good?" Captain Magnus rhetorically asked under his breath.

"Quite," Ficolus answered, "she was a different one."

"How so?" Captain Magnus asked, intrigued, afraid he already knew the answer.

"What is your interest in her, young man?" Ficolus asked, suddenly defensive.

"She's my mother," Captain Magnus answered aggressively.

"An' she's tryin' ta kill us," Balt added.

The old man suddenly stood up and gazed at Captain Magnus with wonder in his eyes, "Yes," he breathed, "yes, I can see the resemblance." he stepped closer, "Do *you* have it as well?"

Rion extended his claws and took a step forward toward the old man.

"Put down the jug, Balt," Meeka warned and got up from her chair.

"But it's so *guid*," Balt began to argue until he saw the tension building around us.

"Please tell me you're not drunk already," Meeka sighed.

"Nope," the dwarf laughed as he gripped his Great Axe, "I'm finally feelin' narmal. I t'ought t'is guy was our friend."

"I *am* your friend," Ficolus cackled, "I just want to know if the boy has the *power*." Ficolus took a step toward Captain Magnus.

"One more step, old man," Rion growled, "and I'll tear you to pieces."

"T'is escalated quickly," Balt chuckled and readied his axe.

"Everyone, take ease." Captain Magnus barked and stood up, his hands waving everyone down, "That's an order."

Everyone complied and slightly relaxed.

"Do they obey you because *of the power?*" Ficolus clawed at the air between he and Captain Magnus.

Rion hissed and began to growl.

"Master?" Navari calmly asked.

Ficolus mindlessly turned and looked at her.

Her eyes were glowing an eerie deep violet, as were the eyes of a few of her snakes, "Tell us about the Grand Ascendancy."

Ficolus dropped to his knees and began to weep, transfixed on Navari's eyes.

"Dammit," Balt cursed quietly under his breath and lowered his axe.

Captain Magnus strafed around to end up standing behind Navari.

"The Grand Ascendancy," Navari repeated.

"Dragons," Ficolus wept uncontrollably, "they're raising dragons."

"Where?" Captain Magnus asked in surprise.

"Haze Mountain," he sobbed.

"The one place we *haven't* checked," Meeka breathed and hammered her right fist into her left hand.

"My mother," Captain Magnus prompted, "is she part of the Grand Ascendancy?"

Without blinking, the old man groaned, "She's their founder and leader."

"I thought so," Captain Magnus replied.

"Can they be stopped?" Navari asked.

"No," Ficolus whined, "it's too late. They already have four juvenile dragons and more babies on the way. Eggs, hundreds of...eggs."

"How do you know all of this?" Meeka asked in shock.

"She was here about a year ago." He blubbered.

"That's about the time she attacked The Scorpion," Captain Magnus calculated, "where is she now?"

"I don't know," Ficolus answered, tears running down his cheeks.

"Sleep," Navari ordered the old wizard.

Ficolus dropped to the floor and began to snore.

Her eyes returned to blackness.

"We should go," Captain Magnus suggested as he threw a few fresh pieces of wood on the old man's fire, "that should keep him warm until he wakes up."

"T'anks fer t'e booze," Balt laughed and set the jug near the old man.

"Maybe he'll wake up and see the jug, thinking he drank too much and passed out," Rion giggled and walked toward the door.

"One can only hope," Captain Magnus said as he closed the door behind him and led the team back down the stairs.

Balt suddenly began to laugh for no apparent reason as soon as they arrived at the bottom of the stairs.

"What's so funny, Balt?" Rion asked.

"Cirdan should come here," Balt gagged on his laughter.

Meeka and Rion joined in on the laughter as Captain Magnus and the now de-hooded Navari just looked at each other and sighed.

CHAPTER SEVEN

MU DHEIREADH BEAGAN SABAID

Back aboard The Scorpion, Captain Magnus ordered the helmsman to take us to find The Dragonfly.

We all sat in the mess hall while the ground team explained what had happened.

I found it amazing how well everyone on the crew had almost immediately accepted Navari as 'safe to look at.'

In the light, we discovered that Navari's eyes were, in fact, violet, her tongue was forked, just like a snake, and up close, her skin was actually covered with flesh-colored scales.

"Now that my secret is out," Navari breathed, "I can assume my natural eating habits."

"Natural eating habits?" Cook asked from the kitchen.

"Rodentia and small mammals," Navari answered.

"No problem," Cook sighed in relief, smacked a rat over the head with a frying pan and held it up by the tail, "dinner is served."

"*Live,*" she smiled with a flick of her tongue.

Cook dropped the rat and frowned.

"Captain," a young sailor burst into the room, "you're wanted on the bridge."

"Is there a problem, Crewman?" Captain Magnus asked as he followed the boy out the door and up the steps.

"Look!" the crew member said and pointed out to sea.

The sun was setting, and it was getting difficult to see.

Out on the horizon, a ship boasting Guadium colors was firing her cannons at an enormous sea monster.

Her sails were all but destroyed and she was leaning to one side as if she might have been taking on water.

"Captain Magnus!" Meeka cried, "They're from Guadium; we *have to help them!*"

"*Listen up!*" Captain Magnus yelled, gaining the crew's attention, "*All hands-on deck and prepare for a rescue mission!*"

"*Battle stations!*" Meeka shouted and the crew began to scuttle.

"*Arrrgggghhh!*" Balt roared, tightened his grip on his Great Axe and ran to the front of the ship, "It be about bloody time."

"Someone man the harpoon!" a sailor shouted.

"I'm on it!" Roash yelled as she sprinted for the weapon.

"Archers," Loher shouted, "with me!"

Lybiidae stepped forward, next to Loher as a large group of sailors scattered and then gathered with her moments later, armed with bows and quivers, Captain Magnus arrived a few moments later, also armed with Loher's old bow she had given him.

She spotted the bow and smiled, "Let the bow do the work," she advised.

Captain Magnus nodded and grinned.

The Scorpion sped toward the ship in need and circled around to the rear of the attacking creature.

"Fire harpoon!" Captain Magnus ordered.

"Aye, Captain," Roash roared, "firing harpoon!" She aimed at the creature's neck and pulled the trigger.

The harpoon sailed through the air and found purchase in the sea monster's skull.

The rope pulled taut, and we felt a violent jerk.

"Use that to swing to its side," Captain Magnus yelled to the helmsman.

The helmsman smiled and nodded as he turned the wheel against the wake and simply skipped The Scorpion around to the side of the creature.

"Fire starboard cannons!" he yelled down the stairs.

"Fire starboard cannons," a voice repeated just before The Scorpion let loose her load with a loud boom.

The blast lit up the darkening sky.

The cannonballs created bloody masses across the creature's side and neck, causing it to abandon its feud with the smaller vessel and turn its attention to The Scorpion.

"Let loose!" Loher commanded as the archers released their arrows into the neck of the foe.

The ship from Guadium quickly retreated and began to circle around to the other side.

"Fire at will," Loher shouted as a stream of flaming arrows began to launch, lighting up the sky.

Suddenly, we heard more cannon blasts.

I looked around to the other side of The Scorpion and caught a glimpse of The Dragonfly, smoke pluming from her cannon ports and flaming arrows flying over her railings.

The creature howled out in pain and tried to dive under the surface, but our harpoon cable wouldn't let it go too deep.

The creature pulled at the cable, trying to pull The Scorpion under with it, but to no avail.

The creature was only tiring itself out.

Several cannon blasts from the other two ships later, and the creature was dead.

Cheers arose from the decks of all three ships as The Scorpion swung around to rest, side by side with The Dragonfly.

The ship from Guadium's captain and crew yelled out their thanks and appreciation before slowly sailing away, back to Guadium.

"Meet us at Avilyn Harbor," Meeka yelled over to The Dragonfly.

"We'll see you there!" Tybidon yelled back.

As The Scorpion sailed past the damaged ship, we tossed out a line and towed them as far as the harbor.

Several hours later, just as the sun was about to rise, the three ships docked at Avilyn Harbor and another thunderstorm was on its way in.

Those of us from each ship arrived indoors as the rain began pouring down in sheets, "We have got a lot of news for you!" Captain Magnus said as he shook Captain Rina's hand.

"Captain Waxx decided not to join us?" Captain Rina asked as she noticed he was not with us, "Is he ill?"

"No, he's retired," Meeka laughed.

A bolt of lightning pierced the sky.

"I thought you were going to say he's dead," Tybidon chuckled.

His comment was ignored, only answered by the rumbling of thunder.

"I'm the new captain of The Scorpion," Captain Magnus proudly announced.

"Aren't you a little young to be a ship's captain?" Rina asked, looking the young man up and down.

"That's exactly what *I* said," Lybiidae giggled.

Another flash of lightning.

"Age is irrelevant," Navari defended, "he's a very good captain."

"I trust your word, Navari," Rina smiled, "so nice to see your face once again."

Rumbling of thunder.

"If he's a 'very good' captain now," Tybidon commented, "imagine 'how good' he will be with some more experience."

Another, closer lightning flash lit the room.

"Am I detecting jealousy in your voice, Commander Trislee?" Navari asked, her eyes flickering.

"A bit," Tybidon admitted and yanked his view away from Navari's gaze, "Dammit, Navari," he cursed, "don't *do* that!"

The thunder was growing louder.

"I see you're going to become an important member of our crew," I said directly, "If you choose to stay."

She turned and looked at me, "I feel more...appreciated aboard The Scorpion," she said.

Captain Rina looked hurt.

The thunder continued.

"With all due respect, Captain Rina," Navari began, "Your crew are a bunch of misguided misfits, while Captain Magnus' crew are more like...family."

Tybidon began to argue, but Captain Rina cut him off, "No Commander, she's right," Captain Rina admitted, "we act more like pirates than a civilized crew."

"An' we be t'e pirates," Balt softly chuckled.

"You see?" Navari asked, trying not to giggle at Balt's comment.

A window sprung open, allowing the rain in, drenching the floor.

Men nearby quickly closed and locked the window shut.

"We're not here to fight," Captain Magnus stepped in, "we're here to ask for your help."

A flash of lightning and almost immediate thunder.

"It's got to be big if you're asking for *our* help," Tybidon sneered.

"*Commander*, report back to the ship and *stay confined to your quarters*." Captain Rina scolded, "That's a *direct* order. Cyrus, go with him and *make* him comply."

"Ooo, you're in trouble now," Cyrus, a large lump of sailor laughed, grabbed the commander by his jacket collar and roughly escorted him out the door.

The door opened just as a bolt of lightning lit up the outside world and closed along with the thunder... 'slam.'

The sun was trying to peek out from behind the storm clouds, diluting the periodic lightning.

"My deepest apologies," Captain Rina bowed, "sometimes he acts like such a toddler and others, like an intelligent man. I don't get it."

"Per'aps 'e's 'ad too many blows to t'e dome," Balt said as he knocked on his helmet.

Rolling thunder seemed to grow with every knock.

"You said you need our help, Captain?" she blinked.

"Yes, we've discovered where the Grand Ascendancy has a sort of base of operations," Captain Magnus smiled.

"And you want our help to attack it?" Rina asked with a laugh.

"NO," Captain Magnus breathed and ushered us into a more secure corner.

"Thar be ***dragons!***" Balt leaned in and whispered with wide eyes, his breath smelled of whisky and tooth decay.

An awkward moment of silence passed.

"Oh, sorry," Captain Rina excused herself, "I was waiting for Commander Trislee to comment," she explained, "something stupid like, 'shut up,' or 'no way,'" she laughed, embarrassed and rambling, "but I just had him arrested, so, no stupid comment."

Balt cleared his throat, cutting her off and repeated, "**Dragons...**"

"Yeah, Balt," Captain Magnus frowned, "we heard you, but Commander Trislee spoiled it for you."

"And he wasn't even here to do it," Navari giggled.

"Do you see what I have to put up with?" Rina groaned.

"I don't miss it," Navari replied with a more serious tone.

"Anyway, back to why you need us," Rina drew the conversation, "you can't seriously think you can take on a dragon, do you?" she asked, "Scorpion or not, a dragon will destroy you and any chance of rebuilding The Scorpion."

"Oh, ye of little faith," Captain Magnus countered, "Nitch," he called.

"Reporting as ordered, Captain," Nitch giggled as he leapt from Navari's hood and landed on the table.

"Are you ready to play, Buddy?" Captain Magnus asked.

Captain Rina began to scoff.

"Euka," Captain Magnus called, "Is jy gereed om te speel, Meisie?"

Euka gently nudged his hand with her nose and began to purr.

Playing, Nitch let out a loud shriek and began to run away from the caracal.

Euka roared and took off after him, batting at him with clawless paws.

The natural errford defenses kicked in, surrounding Nitch in an energy orb, and again, Euka was essentially just playing with a ball.

Her claws came out, yet they never touched Nitch.

She batted him all around the lounge as we continued to talk.

Captain Rina shook her head, trying not to laugh and said, "I don't get it."

"Give them a moment to play and then I'll show you something else." Captain Magnus laughed as Euka and Nitch careened through the lounge.

"Weeee!" Nitch laughed as Euka pounced and batted him into a corner.

"Bring hom terug, asseblief," I called out to Euka, who in turn, batted Nitch toward me and settled him at my foot, "Goeie meisie."

"Well, *that's* impressive, to say the least," Captain Rina commented, amused.

Euka sauntered back to Lybiidae and laid down near her feet.

"Rion," Captain Magnus called, "do you want to take this one?"

Rion nervously stepped forward and patted his hip.

Nitch leapt up to his hip and climbed up to Rion's shoulder, making the giant cat wiggle, giggle, and purr.

Lybiidae produced her bow of accuracy and the recognizable arrows of seeking.

"Do you recognize these?" the Drow asked.

"I do," Captain Rina answered, "a bow of accuracy and I believe those are arrows of searching?"

Lybiidae raised her bow and notched an arrow to the string, "Seeking," she corrected.

"What did I say?" Captain Rina rhetorically asked.

"The leg," Rion begged, "aim for the leg."

Lybiidae took aim...at his chest.

Captain Rina finally looked nervous and intrigued.

Rion closed his eyes, held his breath, and swallowed hard.

...and let her arrow loose.

A massive blue orb suddenly engulfed the eline warrior where he stood.

The arrow bounced off and retreated to Lybiidae's quiver.

Captain Rina's jaw dropped to the table in awe.

"That orb will encase an entire ship," Captain Magnus laughed.

Rina blinked a few times and tried to make sense of what she had just seen, "You've *done this* already?" she asked.

Captain Magnus nodded affirmation as Nitch hopped up, perched on Balt's helmet, and smiled proudly.

"Are there more of these..."

"Errfords, Ma'am," Navari directed.

"Yes, errfords," Captain Rina agreed and nodded at her former crewmate.

"There are," Captain Magnus answered, "however, they're all in a different realm."

"There are more eline there too," Roash added.

"What are we waiting for?" Captain Rina asked excitedly, "We should stock up on provisions and depart immediately."

Captain Magnus laughed, "It's not *that* easy," he said, "We can only take one ship, and there's a lot of magic involved."

"Aw, *dammit!*" the portman cursed.

We looked at him in curiosity.

"What's wrong?" Meeka asked.

"They're back again," he moaned and pointed through the window.

The rain had stopped quite a while ago and now a dense fog had begun to creep out of the sea and rapidly spread across the ground.

The portman was rushing around, locking all the doors and windows.

"Vampires?" I asked, slightly excited.

"No, thank the gods," he chuckled, seeming a bit more at ease, "Skeletons. Hundreds of them," he explained, "they wreak havoc on the docks and try to come in, so I lock the doors."

"How often does this happen?" Loher asked.

"A few times a month," he answered as the army of skeletons began to scratch and bang on the doors and windows.

"Skeletons don't just animate by themselves," Lybiidae commented.

"A Necromancer?" Meeka hypothesized.

"I'm sure of it," Lybiidae smiled.

"Are ye t'inkin' wot I be t'inkin'?" Balt bellied up to the conversation.

"Target practice," Loher suggested.

"Not a bad idea," Captain Magnus smiled.

"Loher and I will hunt for the necromancer, while the rest of you have fun breaking bones," Lybiidae suggested.

"I'm coming with you girls," Roash purred, "I love a good hunt."

"Count us in as well," Meeka announced as she motioned to Navari, "instead of killing the necromancer...right away, perhaps Navari could get some useful information from them? Maybe they're a part of the Grand Ascendancy."

"Logical and ethical," Lybiidae chuckled, "I like you, Meeka."

"Captain Rina," Roash laughed, "you should join us and make it an all girls' team."

The captain thought about it for a second and agreed, "Oh, why not."

Balt and Rion began to growl with glee as they readied their weapons and ran for the closest door.

Nitch took a chance and jumped onto Euka's back.

Euka bucked hard and sent Nitch up further, closer to her neck.

She began to purr and followed Rion out the door.

Broken bones and rusted weapons already littered the ground just outside of the door.

The sounds of metal-on-metal clashing could be heard but were being drowned out by vicious dwarven war cries, eline hissing and roaring from multiple sources.

I kissed Loher and told her I loved her, drew my sword, smiled, and made my way into battle.

The 'girls' team' was directly on my heels.

Arrows, ice balls and throwing knives began to spew forth as we made our way across the battlefield.

Captain Magnus, his Shino Sutoka Katana drawn and ready, caught up with me and asked, "Are you going to vamp out this time?"

The girls' team cut off to the left, leaving me and Captain Magnus in the middle of a large group of skeletons.

"I never know *when* I'm going to vamp out," I laughed and cut down a foe.

Balt could be heard from within the clatter, "T'at's twelve!"

Captain Magnus bent his knees and dropped down, spinning, his blade cutting through the leg bones of three advancing skeletons.

"Sixteen!" Balt laughed as he dodged the sword of his next victim, "Seventeen!" Another broken skeleton crumbled at his feet.

 "I wish they'd fight back more," Rion roared as he smashed a skeleton with his fist.

The skeleton simply crumbled under the blow.

I kicked another in the chest, and it exploded into a dozen pieces, "Something's not right," I warned.

"You're right," Captain Magnus took the weapon from a skeleton's hand and then pushed it over into a pile of bones.

It stayed there, motionless.

Then, with no warning, the skeleton army stopped where they stood and crumbled.

We heard Roash's roar.

Rion roared back.

Roash returned the final roar, and we began walking in her direction.

"That's quite a system you have there," Captain Magnus laughed, impressed.

Euka and Nitch came literally screaming past us, on their way to the girls.

"At least *someone's* 'avin' fun," Balt growled and kicked a skull that crumbled with the impact.

"It was fun while it lasted," Rion purred, "until they stopped fighting."

We circled around the harbor and continued closer to the sea.

Bones and arrows lie, strewn everywhere.

A group of young sailors were scuttling around, retrieving arrows, and throwing knives; they're not cheap.

"Commander," a sailor called from the rocky shoreline, "I found another one of your knives!"

Small waves were lapping at our feet as we arrived to join the girls' team.

They were standing around a small humanoid, standing waist deep in the water, dressed in purple robes.

Captain Rina was standing behind, holding the figure by the shoulders, while Navari was stooped down in front, her eyes glowing violet.

They must have just been finishing, for as we waded deeper into the sea to get closer, they began to wade back toward us, Roash, carrying the sleeping, purple robed figure like a child.

Rion tiptoed gingerly closer, unsuccessfully trying to avoid getting wet and relieved Roash of her small burden.

"Take her inside," Roash hissed as she bounded out of the water and shook herself dry.

It was beginning to rain again and all three 'cats' made a quick dash for the door.

The rest of us followed suit.

Once inside, Rion put the sleeping figure down near the fire on a makeshift bed of spare blankets.

The harbormaster had arrived and was throwing a fit about the thousands of bones all over outside.

The portman and the ferryman were trying to calm him down, yet all it took was one word from Loher, "Necromancer," she said and pointed at the sleeping figure by the fire.

The three men stopped arguing and looked to where she was pointing.

"Does that mean the skeleton attacks will stop?" the ferryman asked excitedly.

"Skeleton attacks?" the harbormaster asked.

"We've *both* told you about the skeleton attacks," the portman growled at his boss.

Balt cleared his throat, trying to gain the men's attention, but went unheard.

"But you never believed us," the ferryman angrily added, pointing a finger in the harbormaster's face, "Fool."

Balt tried again, "Gentlemans" he coughed, trying not to be rude.

"Would *you* believe it if your laziest employees told you some fantastic..."

"I'm gonna bite the next man that speaks," Roash quietly stated with a song in her voice.

Silence.

Roash smiled and licked her teeth at the men.

"T'ank ye, Lass," Balt chuckled, "Aye, t'e stories of t'e skeletons be true," he began, "Ye kin see t'e bones right out t'ere." The dwarf splayed his hand to the window, "But we killt t'em all."

"This is the necromancer that was controlling them," Navari added, hood up, kneeling next to the sleeping body.

"Is it *dead?*" the harbormaster asked in disgust.

"No," Navari began but was cut off.

"Why *not?*" the harbormaster spewed.

Roash hissed at him and splayed her claws in his direction.

"Request permission to take her back to The Scorpion, Captain," Navari asked Captain Magnus.

"Granted." Captain Magnus smiled and then looked over at Meeka, "Commander, would you please do the honors?"

"All aboard that's coming aboard," Meeka giggled and stepped close to Navari and the sleeping necromancer.

"Nitch," Navari called, "I'd like you to join me," she stated.

Lybiidae, Euka and Nitch all decided to go back.

I stepped into the circle and looked at Loher.

"Go ahead," she urged, "I'll stay with the captain."

I blew her a kiss as the pink smoke surrounded us.

⸺◆⸺

Sailors were still throwing bones overboard, while others were mopping up blood from the deck.

"What happened here?" I asked without thinking.

Our battle with the skeletons was foreseen and controlled, while the battle aboard The Scorpion came as a surprise.

"Skeletons, Sir," a sailor answered.

"Did we lose anyone?" I asked.

"No, Sir," he answered, "They took us by surprise and 'Ducky' took a blade to the arm," he pointed to where the blood was, "but 'Cook' patched him up and sent him back out fighting."

"They sure didn't fight good," a different sailor chuckled on his way past us.

"Yeah," another shouted from above, "too easy."

Navari had already taken our guest down below, I excused myself from the crew and followed her.

I was just poking my head into Navari's quarters when we could hear the rest of the team clamoring aboard.

"Perhaps we should wait for everyone else?" Navari suggested.

I nodded and went back up to welcome everyone back.

The blood and bones were completely gone, as if nothing had ever happened.

Captain Magnus, Meeka, and I squeezed into Navari's quarters while everyone else loitered just outside the door.

"Nitch," Navari said, "I need Nitch to translate for me."

"Where's Nitch?" Rion asked from the doorway.

Nitch hopped over the team from head-to-head, settling on my shoulder.

"A translator?" I asked, "What is she?"

Navari removed the small figure's hood, revealing the face of a young female goblin.

A collective breath of wonder echoed through the room.

Goblins were a rare sight in Beornan Heafod, and a female, even rarer.

Rarer still, than even the Drow.

Balt pushed his way closer to take a look, "Awe," he breathed, "she be *beautiful!*" he wept.

Balt was literally crying at the sight of the goblin as he pushed back out of the room.

We all looked at the goblin and then looked around at each other in confusion.

"Can you translate Goblish?" Navari finally asked.

"I can try," the errford admitted, "I didn't know I could speak Elven, or Dwarven, or even Human until I did it," he giggled.

"Can you understand me?" she asked in Medusan.

"I'm honestly not surprised that I can," Nitch giggled back in Medusan.

"Good," she said, in Common to the room, "this will work." She smiled and flicked her tongue, "I'm going to wake her up now."

Navari slowly closed her normally dead-black eyes, and when she snapped them back open, they were glowing an eerie violet, as were most of her snakes' eyes.

The goblin began to stir.

Navari narrowed her focus.

The goblin opened her eyes, took a quick look around at the strange creatures surrounding her, began to try to wiggle free but caught a glimpse of Navari's gaze and became entranced.

"What is your name?" Navari asked.

"I don't understand! Let me go!" Nitch translated, then soothingly asked her for her name in Goblish.

The gobbling stopped wiggling and calmed down a bit, looking for the person that spoke.

"Can you tell me your name?" Nitch asked, making sure he had her attention.

Amused, she looked at what she thought was an odd looking, talking squirrel and giggled, "My name is Ivyroot Thistlebutt, what's yours?"

Navari found that she didn't have to coax the truth out of the young goblin, so she let Nitch take over.

"I'm called, Nitch," he answered, "can you tell me why you animated all of those skeletons?"

"The crazy human lady is holding my family hostage and told me to scare the harbormaster and everyone away so she can live at the harbor," she answered all in one breath.

Meeka began to usher all nonessential personnel out of the room, including me, leaving Captain Magnus, Nitch, and a hidden Navari alone and in comfort.

I listened in at the door.

Euka had somehow snuck back into the room and curled up gently beside Ivyroot; she was gently running her fingers through the caracal's soft fur as she interacted with Nitch.

"Do you like the crazy human lady?" Nitch asked.

Thankfully, she answered, "No, she's mean and has my mom and dad in prison until I scare everyone away from the harbor."

Brown smoke suddenly began to circle Ivyroot, but Captain Magnus thought fast and put a quick Psi-dome around her, cutting off the intrusive blink spell attempt.

"I have a bad feeling we're about to have company," I breathed to the rest of the team.

"Mom," Captain Magnus called to Meeka, "you and Nitch, help Navari keep an eye on her incase anything happens, Rion, Balt, stay here at the door and stop anyone from getting in here, the rest of you, spread out with bows and Roash...do whatever it is that you do."

Roash smiled, showing her razor-sharp teeth, and disappeared into the shadows of the hold.

Meeka had a worried look on her face as she closed and locked the cabin door.

Loher and I put our hoods up and stationed ourselves within line of sight of Navari's cabin doorway, while Lybiidae, already partially shadowed, also strung up her bow and disappeared.

Captain Magnus ran up the stairs to the upper deck to warn the rest of the crew.

"What's happening?" Ivyroot asked, terrorized.

"We're trying to keep you safe from the crazy human lady," Nitch soothed.

"Is she here?" she whimpered.

"Not yet," Nitch whispered and tried to make her comfortable.

A few moments later, shouting, growling, crashing and loud thuds could be heard just outside the door.

***

It didn't take long, after the entire team was poised and ready for the attack, for the brown smoke to form in several separate locations aboard The Scorpion.

"Here we go, Scorpion!" Captain Magnus heroically cried and drew his katana, lunging at the first figure to step out of the smoke.

It was a hobgoblin, cut down before it could even gain its bearings.

Within seconds, the deck was infested with orcs and hobgoblins, the crew fighting with everything they had.

The Scorpion crew began to overpower the marauders and gained the upper hand.

From below, vicious roars and clashing could be heard, echoing up the stairs.

Captain Magnus could see that his crew had the enemy managed well enough for him to head below and help keep Ivyroot safe.

As he entered the hold, bodies of hobgoblins and orcs were already piled up on the deck, most with an arrow or two jutting out of them.

The wooden floor was slippery with blood, making proper footing difficult.

Balt was standing atop a pile of bodies, swinging his Great Axe at a group of marauders trying to breach Navari's door.

Suddenly, a hand and arm reached out from within a pile of the dead and grabbed the leg of an orc, dragging it in to its death.

Lybiidae appeared next to the pile and smiled, "I didn't think that would work!" she stated proudly.

"That was you?" I asked, slightly horrified, pointing to where the arm reached out.

"Yeah," she laughed, "watch."

Rion had a dozen or so orcs trapped in a corner, playing with them, amusing himself, so we waited until he 'accidentally' let one slip past him and Lybiidae nodded at the pile of corpses closest to the escapee.

Another butchered arm reached out from the middle of the pile and grabbed the dumbfounded beast by the ankle and pulled hard.

As the creature went down, another, knife wielding hand plunged a blade into the skull of its victim.

Dead.

"That's just *creepy*." I smiled and thwapped an arrow into the side of an orc's head as it evaded Captain Magnus's katana and tried to return attack.

The last remaining foes were two humans that had surrendered to us almost immediately.

Roash had them under guard in her quarters.

Captain Magnus lightly knocked on Navari's door, "We won," he whispered.

The bolt slid open, and the door cracked open a bit.

He opened the door slowly and peeked inside, "Is she okay?" he asked.

Meeka smiled, "Other than a bunch of loud banging, roaring and screaming from out there," she said, "it was calm and peaceful in here."

"Keep her in here while we..." he paused, thinking, "tidy up a bit out here?"

"Take your time," Meeka smiled, "she's playing with Euka right now. We'll be fine."

"Is she hungry?" Captain Magnus asked.

Meeka asked into the room and then answered, "A bit, mostly thirsty."

"Water and...what?" Captain Magnus asked.

"Raw meats an' roots," Balt answered behind him, "raw meats we got," he said and pointed at the dead bodies, "but roots..."

"You start," Captain Magnus gulped, "carving up the meat and I'll go fetch the water." He raced around the corner to the mess hall.

"Don't mind if I do," Rion licked his chops, began to purr, and drew his sword.

Balt couldn't look and turned away, "Disgustin'."

"Orc is just pork without all the P," Rion purred and sank his blade into a severed arm.

"Gross."

As Ivyroot, Rion, Roash and Navari shared their meal of potatoes and orc, the rest of us went to Roash and Meeka's cabin and interrogated the humans.

Captain Magnus put a Psi dome around The Scorpion to deter any unwanted blink spells or intruders as we sailed for The Scorpion's Den.

We had to get there before Captain Magnus's limited energy ran out.

CHAPTER EIGHT

YOU CAN RUN...

The Scorpion disappeared into the hidden cave, now called The Scorpion's Den, while The Dragonfly cruised around the area keeping an eye out for any sign of the enemy.

The only way into the subterranean cove was to have The Scorpion actually walk over a few meters of dry land and settle back into a deep lagoon within the cave.

It was impossible for any other ship to enter unless strong magic was involved.

We felt safe there, safer than anywhere else in the realm, and with a temporary Psi dome over the cave, we felt untouchable.

Even without Kuchoff's Psi-dome, we were still extremely safe, as we had purchased a few heavy cannons that were strategically placed around the hidden cove.

Crew members in rotating shifts watch from other strategic locations atop the mountain with easy access to alarm those inside with whistles.

It was virtually an impenetrable fortress.

We unloaded our new prisoners and put them each in their own cell of the brig Balt had built within the walls of the Hollow.

They were secure and undetectable, according to Captain Magnus, who had sailed around the island trying to detect them using every means he had available, thankfully, to no avail.

We had also informed His Majesty of the situation.

The King agreed that the prisoners would be safer incarcerated within the Hollow than anywhere else, and that he and Avilyn would arrive promptly for a proper interrogation.

"I guess it's 'hurry up and wait' time," I groaned and slumped into a chair by the fire.

"Are you hungry?" Loher asked, looking up from her fletching.

"No," I sighed, "I'm bored."

"Why don't you go see what Balt is up to?" she suggested, "I'm sure he and Rion are up to something amiss."

"You're a great influence," I said, sarcastically, kissed her head and went searching for Balt.

It didn't take long for the sound of laughter and commotion to be heard, echoing across the hollow cove.

I smiled, quickened my pace, and went to investigate.

As I narrowed in on the laughter and noises, I saw a group of crew members gathered, circling around some sort of action.

It reminded me of so many years ago, when I witnessed a group of fairies riding rabbits in a race around a tree.

Whatever it was, I wanted a piece of the action.

I casually walked up on the group, "What's going on, guys?"

A few of the crew members looked a little anxious with my presence, "They were already dead, Sir," one of them blurted out, pointing into the circle.

My eyes followed in his finger's direction to a dozen or so dead rats, strewn around the center of the circle of crew members.

A few of them were quite mangled.

Suddenly, Balt arrived with a few more dead rats and tossed them into the circle.

Then I noticed Nitch and Ivyroot among the crew members.

I began to smile because I was fairly sure I knew what was happening here, but decided to wait and see if I was correct.

"Go ahead," I prompted; Nitch translated, and Ivyroot began to chant and move her hand in odd formations.

The dead rats began to move.

Slowly, at first, but after a brief time, they began behaving as if they were still alive.

Balt began to chuckle as random crew members began throwing darts at the reanimated rats.

The rats began dodging the darts as if they were self-aware, yet one by one the rats found themselves tacked to the floor, dead...again.

"It be like target practice," Balt chuckled oddly, as if trying to excuse any wrongdoings.

"I think it's a good idea," I commented, "just clean up after yourselves and don't get in anyone's way."

"Aye, Sir," a few crew members affirmed.

From the mountain peak lookout came three sharp whistles.

"Friendly ship ahoy," a crew member called out.

'Probably the King and Avilyn,' I thought to myself and strolled out to the lagoon.

I could see The Dragonfly and a small Royal yacht sailing toward the Den.

As the two vessels drew closer, Avilyn, the King and four Royal guards blinked into the cave and the two ships sailed on and away as if nothing ever happened.

"Your Majesty, Avilyn," I greeted as Avilyn's smoke dissipated, "welcome back to The Scorpion's Den."

"I see you've been busy," the King smiled as he noticed all the construction we had done over the past two years.

A complete small town had been built within the interior of the cave.

"I hear you've been busy as well," I laughed and pointed at his wedding ring.

The King smiled from ear to ear.

"I'm afraid we have much uncomfortable news for you, my Liege," Captain Magnus somberly announced as he walked up to us.

"Ah, Captain," the King smiled and greeted Captain Magnus, "bad news you say?"

"We have a few prisoners that Navari has interrogated," Captain Magnus began.

"She's something else, isn't she?" the King smiled, "Please continue."

"Well, M'lord, according to the prisoners, all from the Grand Ascendancy, they're raising dragons somewhere on Haze Mountain."

The King's smile faded, "Dragons?" he finally laughed in disbelief.

"That's the report," Captain Magnus groaned, "we caught a goblin that was animating skeletons at Avilyn Harbor, trying to scare everyone away so Amaliya could take the harbor over as her own."

"*My* harbor??" Avilyn growled, visually angry.

"You own that harbor?" I asked.

"I do," Avilyn answered gruffly, fuming, "where is this... goblin?"

"Right this way," Captain Magnus motioned and began to lead the way.

We walked up on the circle of crew members surrounding the pile of reanimated rats.

Nitch and Ivyroot were standing in the middle.

"Nitch," I began, "We need to talk to Ivyroot."

Without warning, Avilyn pushed his way through the crowd, roughly snatched Ivyroot up by the scruff of her neck and violently threw her across the room.

Ivyroot soared through the air and crashed to a stop against the far wall.

Where a goblin should have been, on the floor under the impact site, lay Lemac Conall, the wizard we had captured twice before.

Speaking for myself, (and I'm sure anyone else that witnessed this,) my shock and anger at Avilyn's actions suddenly turned to Lemac.

Lemac shook off his potential injuries, stood up, smiled wildly, and drew his sword.

Before anyone could react, Avilyn had produced a flaming sword from perhaps somewhere within his robes, and began running at the wizard, screaming out an ancient elven battle cry.

As if hypnotized by the battle cry, Roash and Rion sprang into action and circled around the pair of combatants.

The two swords clashed sending sparks in every direction.

Strike after strike, they couldn't get the upper hand on the other.

Avilyn let out another elven battle cry, different than the last, and Rion thrust in and attacked with his short sword.

Lemac narrowly dodged the eline blade and kicked at Avilyn, landing a boot square in the old elf's chest, knocking him down.

Roash sprang forward and clawed at the human's face and neck, attempting to claw out his eyes and throat.

Her claws ripped off a chunk from the left side of his head, including his ear.

He screamed out in pain as blood began to pour down to his shoulder.

She spat his ear back at him as he tried to regain his focus.

Arrows suddenly began to emerge from the direction of my house; Loher had arrived.

Unfortunately, her arrows were deflected by Lemac's blade and bounced harmlessly onto the floor.

Then, another familiar war cry erupted as Balt and his Great Axe bound into the fray, "Ye was s'posta be a *beautiful goblin girl!*" he cried, but the wizard simply lobbed an ice ball at the dwarf's head.

Splinters of ice exploded off the warrior's helmet, knocking Balt off course, losing momentum.

The dwarf fell, but immediately rolled back to his feet and continued running at the foe.

Lemac suddenly looked worried as Loher pulled back on her bowstring, Balt was in full charge, Rion and Roash were circling, and Avilyn had just gotten to his feet.

With a mighty roar, Rion grabbed Lemac, just as Loher's arrow plunged into the eline's shoulder, missing its intended target.

Rion hissed and involuntarily let Lemac go.

Balt, unable to stop in time, collided with the fur covered mountain, while Lemac rolled out of the way, laughing hysterically, and clutching at the side of his face.

Avilyn came down with his fiery sword, cleaving only brown smoke as Lemac conveniently blinked away.

"DAMMIT!" Balt cursed as he picked himself up and checked for injuries.

"Nitch," I called out to the room, "tend to the wounded, Loher, come with me!"

I began running to the brig as Loher, Captain Magnus, the King, and his men followed me.

We rounded the corner to find Lemac by the cell doors trying to unlock one.

I drew my own sword and engaged the wizard in battle.

He blocked my first swing, and I blocked his.

His next swing missed my cheek by less than a breath, while my blade found purchase on his well armored thigh, slicing through his purple robe.

He laughed aloud and swung at me again, slicing into my left shoulder, but I felt no pain.

My senses heightened and I knew I was...

"He's about to vamp out!" Captain Magnus beamed.

"Vamp?" a Royal guard asked, "As in, vampire?"

"Just watch," Captain Magnus grinned his toothy grin.

I could feel the blood trickle down my arm as I swung my blade at the wizard.

Again, my blade contacted his heavily armored chest, but harmlessly bounced off.

Lemac found an opening and thrust his sword through my abdomen and twisted his blade.

I felt no pain as I dropped my sword and grabbed him by the throat with both hands.

I began to squeeze with all my strength but found myself gripping my own hand.

Lemac and the other two wizards had vanished within a cloud of smoke.

Two sharp whistles sounded.

"Enemy ship ahoy!" a crew member cried.

"Get to The Scorpion!" Captain Magnus ordered the room and began sprinting toward the ship.

Cannon fire could be heard as The Dragonfly engaged the enemy outside.

Loher and I began to make our way to The Scorpion as Navari, Lybiidae, Euka and Nitch caught up.

"You're wounded!" Navari exclaimed as she saw the stream of blood trailing behind me.

"I'm fine for now," I told her as we continued toward the ship, "you can heal me once we're aboard."

Lybiidae gave Loher a worried look.

"I'll explain everything later," Loher smiled uncomfortably and helped me aboard.

Two minutes later, we had crawled over the land patch and were racing out to help The Dragonfly.

The enemy ship was trying to sail away as fast as the wind could take it, while the much smaller Dragonfly was losing ground and falling behind.

As long as we could still see them, we followed them.

They were heading straight for Haze Mountain.

"Haze mountain is where they are allegedly raising dragons?" Avilyn enquired.

"According to Ivyroot," I paused, "I mean, Lemac, but now, I'm not sure *what* to believe."

"We're going to find out soon enough," Captain Magnus stated, "we're going to follow them until they either disappear, which I'm fully expecting, or they dock somewhere. In that case..." he smiled and fingered the handle of his katana, implying more fighting.

Navari grabbed me from behind and tried to gently ease me into a comfortable position so she could begin healing my wounds.

"I'm in no pain," I laughed as she looked as if she were sympathetically feeling the pain for me.

She looked at me in disbelief, "How can that be?" she asked, "I saw you run through and you're losing a **lot** of blood."

"Thunor is..." Loher began with a slightly nervous laugh, trying to find the right words, "a few years back, he was bitten by a vampire..." she explained the whole thing as best as she could without confusing anyone listening.

"And I thought *I* was the only immortal being among us," Nitch laughed after hearing the tale.

"Virtually immortal," Balt and I playfully corrected.

"They're slowing down, Captain," the helmsman announced.

"Match course and speed, please," Captain Magnus replied, "try not to be seen."

"Aye, Captain."

"I'm sure they know we're out here," the King commented.

"I'm sure you're right, M'lord," Captain Magnus replied, "but they may not know *exactly* where we are."

"They're turning toward Haze Mountain, Sir," the Helmsman announced.

"Circle around the other way and try to cut them off," Captain Magnus replied.

"Aye, Sir."

The Scorpion gently veered off to the right and continued around the southern side of the mountain.

"They've disappeared around the northern side of the mountain, Sir."

"Full stop. Hold position here for a moment, Helm," the captain ordered.

"Holding position here, Sir."

"From our vantage point," Captain Magnus began, "we can see both the western shore and the eastern shore of the mountain island, so if they sail past Haze Mountain, we'll see them, and if we don't, they stopped on the north side of the mountain."

More than enough time had passed for them to sail past the mountain with no sighting.

"The rumors must be true," Captain Magnus smiled, "they stopped at Haze Mountain, Helm, circle around to the north side. Let's see if they're there."

"Circling to the north side, Sir."

We sailed around to the northern side of the island and came up empty.

The enemy ship had, in fact, disappeared, just as Captain Magnus had suspected.

"There's *got* to be a cave or something," Meeka sighed in frustration, "and it's getting too dark to see properly."

"Reverse course and stay out of sight," Captain Magnus commanded.

"Helm," Meeka placed her hand on the helmsman's shoulder, "take us to Guadium, please."

"Aye, Ma'am."

"Guadium?" Navari asked.

"My home," Meeka smiled and then turned to Captain Magnus, "there are a few things I'd like to retrieve. I'm sure we'll need them."

"We've been with each other for countless years," Captain Magnus smiled, "and now you're finally going to show us where you're from?"

"It's never been important until now," she sighed, "we need my tomes." She pantomimed opening a book, "And besides," she laughed, "it was just last autumn the McLaauds finally showed us *their* home."

Loher and I smiled at each other at the sound of 'McLaauds.'

"I went back to the ship," Captain Magnus reminded.

"Not my..." she smiled and kissed him on the forehead, "...fault."

"We're heading down below," Loher giggled and grabbed my arm, "to check on Rion."

We left the bridge.

"You know," I laughed as we walked hand in hand, "you shot me once as well."

"Ugh," Loher grunted, "don't remind me."

"'Don't die,'" I laughed and quickened my pace, so she had to run to catch me.

We were still laughing when we entered the infirmary, "W'at'cha laughin' at?" Balt asked, smiling.

"I was reminding Loher of the time she shot *me*," I chuckled.

"I was juss tellin' ol' Rion 'ere about t'at too!" Balt chortled, making Rion and Roash laugh as well.

"How are you doing, Rion? I'm so sorry..." Loher began.

"I'm okay," Rion cut her off, mid apology, "it was my fault anyway," he moaned, "I should have looked before I moved. I could see you then, as well as I can see you now."

"I just don't understand how the arrow missed his armor," Roash wondered aloud, "and got *between* his plates."

"Lucky shot?" Loher guessed.

"That would be *my* fault," Lybiidae admitted, stepping out from a shadowy corner, "I fletched some Arrows of Seeking for you and put them in your quiver. I'm sorry, I should have told you, but I wanted it to be a surprise."

"Surprise," Rion purred.

"But he deflected my first two arrows," Loher countered.

"Probably two normal arrows still mixed in," I suggested.

Loher and Lybiidae nodded in agreement.

"Can you teach me how to fletch those?" the Seolfer elf asked the Drow elf.

"Sure," the former answered, "come with me."

The pair of she-elves left the room, chatting about fletching and bowstrings, followed by Euka.

"Now, let me see about healing that shoulder," Nitch gurgled as he leapt up to Rion's other shoulder and scurried around the back of his enormous neck.

A quick flash of blue and the rattling of an arrow hitting the deck later, Rion was as good as new.

"Ahh," Rion sighed in relief and rubbed his shoulder, "much better, thank you, my tiny furry friend."

"You're quite welcome, my giant furry friend," Nitch giggled and scampered away.

We could feel the ship slowing down.

"There's no way we're already near Guadium," Loher scoffed playfully and began striding up the stairs.

We arrived above deck just to see Avilyn blink himself, the King, and his guards off The Scorpion and onto the dock at Avilyn Harbor.

I could hear Avilyn happily yell, "It's good to be home!" as we sailed on to Guadium.

"Keep going past that old port," Meeka instructed, "and stop just off the shore of Guadium, we won't be long."

"Blinking, Ma'am?" the helmsman asked.

"That's right, blinking," Meeka giggled, "right in and right out."

"We're not staying for a visit?" Captain Magnus frowned.

"You probably won't want to," Meeka replied dryly.

The ground team consisted of: Meeka, Captain Magnus and Euka, at Meeka's request.

Just a quick in and out.

They blinked directly from The Scorpion to Meeka's kitchen.

The cottage was dank and dusty, with a pile of bones scattered across a rug by the cold fireplace.

She leaned down and plucked an object from within the pile of bones and stuffed it into her bag.

Cobwebs hung from everything available, and the dust was literally four millimeters thick in places.

Captain Magnus looked through the window and saw burned out cottages and collapsing barns.

Overgrown weeds and hedges overtook the walkways and streets.

"What happened here?" Captain Magnus asked in disbelief, "You don't seem upset, so you obviously already knew...Mom, what happened here?"

Meeka turned to look at him, tears welling up in her eyes.

She shook her head as they began to cascade down her cheeks.

Turning away, she blew her nose into an old rag from the table and sobbed, "Your mother happened here," she took a deep breath and continued, "before the King called for us, before I even *knew* you."

"Why?" Captain Magnus asked, "What did she want?"

Meeka was frantically searching her bookcases, carelessly tossing the wrong books to the side, "Here's one," she muttered, "but it's not *the* one, where is it?"

She stuffed the book into her bag and remembered the object from the pile of bones.

"Euka, come here," Meeka coaxed.

The caracal complied.

Meeka strapped the object around the caracal's neck and made a few adjustments, "I'm looking for a tome with green eyes on the spine, can you help me?" Meeka asked.

Euka began to sniff and paw around the cottage as Meeka and Captain Magnus searched the bookcases.

"Found it!" an unfamiliar, muffled voice announced.

Meeka turned to look, "Ahh, Euka, I *knew* you could find it!" she laughed.

Euka dropped the book, "It tastes nasty," the caracal spat.

"Well, it's very old," Meeka giggled.

Captain Magnus dropped the stack of books he was holding and gaped in disbelief at the talking cat, "Now I *have* seen everything."

"It's just the Collar of Familiarity, Silly," she giggled and displayed the collar around Euka's neck.

"Wow! Lybi's going to love it!" Euka cheered.

"Lybi?" Meeka raised an eyebrow.

"Lybiidae," Euka replied, "Lybi is short for Lybiidae."

"I get it," Captain Magnus chuckled.

Meeka smiled, "From now on, she will be, 'Lybi' to me as well."

"What if she hates it?" Euka frowned.

"Don't *you* call her 'Lybi'?" Captain Magnus asked.

"I would have if I could talk to her," Euka purred.

Meeka giggled and sighed, picked up the tome Euka had found and showed it to Captain Magnus, "This is what your mother wanted, but I fought her off. She destroyed half of Guadium before she found me."

"How did she know you had it?" he asked.

"She didn't," Meeka sighed, trying not to break down again, "I was the last person in town that could possibly have it." She coughed, "The last wizard."

"All the rest..." Captain Magnus began.

"She killed," Meeka confirmed.

Captain Magnus's face knotted into a hateful scowl, "No more," Captain Magnus slammed his boot down on the floor, kicking up years of dust, "No More! I swear it now, Mother. You will die by *my hand*."

"But that's your *mother*," Euka started.

"He knows," Meeka soothed, "we've had this same conversation. It won't work."

"Let's get back to The Scorpion," Captain Magnus growled, trying to calm down.

⸺ ⟡ ⸺

The ground team stepped through the rapidly dissipating cloud of pink smoke, "Avilyn Harbor, Helm," Captain Magnus called.

"Aye Captain."

Meeka spotted Lybiidae, "Hey, Lybi, we have a surprise for you."

We all began to gather around.

"Did you just call me, 'Lybi?'" Lybiidae giggled as she stepped nearer.

"Short for Lybiidae, do you like it?" Euka asked.

Without realizing who had asked the question, Lybiidae answered, "Yes! I think it's cute...Wait, *what??*" Lybi screamed, "Did you just *talk?*"

"Look at my new collar!" Euka boasted.

"The collar makes her talk?" Lybi asked with a wide smile.

"Do you like it?" Euka asked.

"I *love it!*" she cried and threw her arms around the caracal.

"All ashore that's goin' ashore," a crew member called as we moored up to the dock at Avilyn Harbor.

Through the window, I could see that Avilyn, the King and company were still there.

The Dragonfly was on a short approach to the dock as well.

"Fancy meeting you here," Captain Rina shouted down from the railing.

"Thanks for the assist yesterday," Captain Magnus returned.

"What are friends for?" she laughed as she deboarded her ship and joined us on the dock.

"You're about to witness a lot of weird stuff," I warned The Dragonfly crew, "try to take it in stride."

"Like what?" Commander Trislee politely asked.

"Like a talking caracal," Euka roared for fun.

Tybidon just bit his upper lip and nodded, trying to retain his composure.

Captain Rina only giggled; about which, I'm not completely sure.

We entered the harbor and attracted immediate attention, "Reunited so soon?" Avilyn greeted us with warmth and sincerity.

"Where is the Harbormaster?" Captain Rina asked.

"Ahh, Grephine," Avilyn cooed, "just the captain I was looking for."

"I'm sorry," Captain Rina commented, "how do you…"

"Know your first name?" he asked for her, "I know many, many things," he laughed, "your name is simply, just one."

"And how may I be of service?" she asked.

"I need a new Harbormaster," the elf replied.

"And you're choosing me?" she asked.

"Can I trust you?" Avilyn asked without blinking.

"I do," Captain Magnus vouched.

"As do I," I vouched.

"What if I don't want the job?" Grephine asked.

"Well, that would be a shame," Avilyn frowned.

"Please, Ma'am," the portman begged.

"It's not as if you have to *be* here all the time," the ferryman added.

"We could use stability, Captain," Commander Trislee mentioned half under his breath.

Captain Rina took a moment and thought about it, "I'll do it," she answered, "as long as I can still hunt Amaliya."

"She wants this place," I mentioned, "chances are, she'll be coming to you...here."

"And we won't be too far away," Captain Magnus added.

"I can station some troops here if you'd like," the King offered.

Captain Rina smiled, "That would be a big help, my Liege."

"How many would you like?" he asked.

"That would be for his Majesty to decide," Rina coyly answered.

The King smiled, "Expect fifty on the morrow, once I return to Salvus Hus."

"You are most gracious, your Highness," Captain Rina habitually bowed.

The King didn't seem to mind.

"Good. Now that that's settled," Avilyn chuckled, "is his Highness ready to return to the Keep?"

"The four of you stay here and protect this harbor," the King commanded the guards and stepped closer to the elven wizard.

Orangish smoke suddenly engulfed the two and they gracefully disappeared.

—◆—

We waited until daybreak to return to Haze Mountain, so we could see if there was some sort of hidden entrance.

Loher, Meeka, and I were settled, up front on the bow.

Meeka was thumbing through her tomes, while Loher was practicing the fletching Lybi had taught her.

I was keeping an eye out for any sign of the Grand Ascendancy.

Haze Mountain was just ahead, about an hour's travel, with no ships of any kind in sight.

The sea was calm and peaceful, and some crew members were taking advantage by fishing; seafood was definitely on the menu tonight.

"How fortunate for us!" Meeka suddenly blurted aloud and retrieved Lemac's wand from within her robes, "This tome describes this exact wand as some sort of key to something," she spewed.

"Are you sure it's that *exact* wand?" I teased.

She stood up, held the tome out for me to see and showed me the wand.

The illustration in the tome and the wand in her hand looked exactly alike, down to the small crease in the gold that held the decorative gems in place.

"Fascinating," I breathed, "keep reading," I urged, "I think you may be getting somewhere with this."

"I'm sure of it," Loher muttered without looking up from her task.

Meeka smiled and sat back down on the deck, studying intently.

We were approaching Haze Mountain from the west, while the Dead Dunelands were to our north.

We decided to keep our distance for a while by staying close to the southern banks of the uninhabitable Dunelands, trying to stay out of sight as much as possible.

The melted sand on the shore looked like glass, and a dragon's skeleton could still be seen half covered by the sand and glass mixture.

The sun was glinting off the shiny surface, making it almost painful to look at.

The Scorpion suddenly began to veer south.

Haze Mountain was about two kilometers away.

We were closing in on it quickly, as the wind, albeit just a light breeze, was in our favor.

Suddenly, the sea, about a half of a kilometer ahead of The Scorpion, began to churn.

"Captain!" a crew member called out with a twinge of fear in his voice.

Captain Magnus poked his head out from the bridge, "I see it," he called back as he began to sprint to the bow to get a better look.

Just as Captain Magnus arrived next to me, giant tentacles began to rise out of the churning sea.

"**Sea monster!**" a few voices called out and the ship began to come alive with bustling crew members.

Captain Magnus began to laugh.

Softly, at first, but his laughter grew stronger, louder, almost intense.

"Captain Magnus?" I asked slightly afraid, due to the sea monster in front of us.

His laughing calmed down to a hearty chuckle.

"Sweetheart," Meeka prodded, "why are you laughing? It's a sea monster!"

His chuckle subsided to coughing giggles, "It's an illusion," he snorted, trying to calm himself, "I recognize the Psi structure of it."

The crew was still scuttling about, awaiting orders from their captain.

"False alarm," Captain Magnus called out to his crew, "it's just an elaborate illusion, we're going to sail right through it."

Uneasily, the crew settled back into their routines, trusting their captain.

The Scorpion sailed, just as Captain Magnus had expected, right through the terrifying illusion that Amaliya had left as a deterrent.

A small cheer arose from around the ship once it was established that we were, in fact, safe.

Haze Mountain was just a few meters away at this time and we all began looking for an entrance to a hidden cave, like that of The Scorpion's Den.

Meeka, Nitch, and Navari were pouring over the wand and tomes, gleaning bits and pieces of useful information.

We orbited the island about a half dozen times, searching for different signs of anything unnatural or out of place.

As we circled back around and found ourselves at the northernmost end of the island, Nitch, exhausted from translating one of the tomes, sat down on the wand, as if it were a bench and thought of his home in Errfordland.

The green eyes on the spine of one of the tomes began to glow and then flipped into the air and landed on the deck, open to a page with a map and an ancient language.

The tome continued to glow a brilliant emerald green.

"I recognize this map," I said as I studied the writing on the page, "but I can't make out the words."

"I recognize it as well," Loher acknowledged.

Nitch suddenly realized that it was a map of Errfordland, "How strange is it," he began, still resting on the wand, "that I was just daydreaming of my home?"

"Object ahoy!" a crew member shouted, "Port side!"

We all looked to the left of the ship and scanned the area.

"A portal!" Lybiidae shouted and pointed at the shoreline.

"It looks like it's closing." Meeka frowned as she ran to get closer.

"We'll catch the next one," Captain Magnus laughed.

"Next one?" Meeka questioned.

"Someone figured something out," Captain Magnus explained, "and I figure with some further trial and error, we should be able to figure out what was figured out."

"I saw where the portal was," I commented and pointed between two obviously placed rocks just offshore, "perhaps if we hold our position near it, we could trigger it again," I suggested.

"Exactly what I was thinking," Captain Magnus smiled and tapped the side of his head with a finger, "Helm, hold position facing between those two pointy rocks. Stay about five meters away."

"Aye, Sir."

The Scorpion swung around and positioned herself how the captain wanted.

"In position and holding, Sir," the helmsman announced.

Captain Magnus led the team back to the bow of the ship, where Meeka, Nitch and Navari were still hovering over the tomes.

"It *can't* be *that* easy," Meeka snorted and closed the green-eyed tome, setting it on the deck.

"Meeka?" Captain Magnus asked, eager for her reply.

"I hope this works," she said as she stood in front of the tome with the green eyes on the spine,

palmed the wand and closed her eyes.

Almost instantly, the tome glowed green, flipped up into the air and landed open to the same map of Errfordland.

The tome lay silent, glowing on the deck.

"Portal!" Lybi called out, pointing between the two rocks.

"Helm," Captain Magnus yelled, "Full Ahead!"

The Scorpion lurched forward and sailed right into the portal.

CHAPTER NINE

TAKING STOCK

The unmistakable shoreline of Errfordland suddenly appeared before us and we were coming in fast.

The helmsman violently cranked the wheel to the right and barely managed to steer The Scorpion away from the treacherous rocks we had impaled ourselves on the first time we arrived here.

Years had passed and it looked as though nothing had changed as we slipped into the natural bay by our old beach.

The sand was still stained red in places from all the blood lost in the multiple battles we had fought here.

The helmsman anchored The Scorpion in her usual resting place and the crew began to disembark to shore.

"Aww," Balt chuckled, "nobody be 'ere ta greet us."

Rion and Roash reached the beach and began striding back toward the clearing in which the eline camp was stationed.

Rion let out a deafening roar and slowly continued walking.

A return roar could be heard in the direction we were walking.

Roash sang out the customary third call and we quickened our pace.

As we entered the forest and followed the path to the clearing, dozens of eline suddenly began to emerge and greet us warmly.

Without making an actual count, I could see that most of the eline had an errford companion.

It was pleasing to see the two species coexisting peacefully.

After a quick exchange of pleasantries, the eline escorted us to the camp.

Upon entering the clearing, more eline and errfords greeted us and welcomed us back.

A large figure emerged from the main tent and began to slowly walk toward us.

The sun was already quite low in the sky, descending behind the figure, making it impossible to make out any features; just the lumbering, hulking shape moving toward us.

It suddenly began to sprint toward us, coming in at breakneck speed.

Closer...

Faster...

I tensed up and braced for impact, but...

I felt a slap on the back of my head as laughter erupted all around us.

"You need your own errford, Pal," Cirdan's voice cut through the laughter.

I looked up and saw the face of my old...friend.

Scarred and ugly, missing a tooth, half an ear and a few whiskers, his face was like a warm...slap on the back of the head.

"Look at your boy!" the eline leader exclaimed, "he's a *grown man!*"

"He's also the captain of The Scorpion," Meeka proudly announced.

A scattered cheer arose from the ranks.

"The *captain!*" Cirdan roared in delight and confusion, "is Waxx *dead?*"

"No," Captain Magnus answered, "Retired."

"Better off dead," Cirdan chuckled under his breath and raised a clawed paw-hand, "Let's celebrate the return of our friends!" he ordered, "and the man that now leads them!"

Collective roars could be heard across the clearing.

Captain Magnus boldly put his arm around Cirdan's shoulder and began to lead him to the command tent, "Come my friend," he said with a toothy grin, "we have much to discuss."

Cirdan smiled and allowed himself to be led; the two leaders slipped away into the command tent.

⚬

The festivities carried out until the last of us crawled back to the ship and passed out from exhaustion, including Rion and Balt.

I found it surprising that both Roash and Rion chose to sleep aboard The Scorpion, rather than in their own beds in the camp.

Perhaps the years of rocking back and forth on a ship is as comforting to them as it is to me.

I still can't sleep well without rocking back and forth.

I digress.

The familiar birdsongs of the island were a welcomed change first thing in the morning, and I arose feeling fine and refreshed.

Nitch was even literally bright eyed and bushy tailed, scampering along with a few other errfords.

Cook already had some coffee made and I eagerly grabbed a cup.

Standing on the deck of The Scorpion with a cup of fresh coffee, looking out over the now familiar land we were once prisoners on, was admittedly something I had never expected, nor hoped for, but something I completely enjoyed.

The only part that was missing was...

"Good morning, My Love," Loher sang just before she kissed me and stole my cup of coffee, "I missed this place."

She closed her eyes and sniffed the coffee, the sun, bathing her face in an angelic glow, "It's so quiet and peaceful here," she breathed and took another sip before handing the cup back to me.

We stood there in relative silence, watching the sea birds soar over the waves.

Meeka and Lybi were strolling on the beach, enjoying the sun; Euka, batting her Nitch-In-A-Ball around, not too far from them.

Errfords were skittering around them as they played.

Every so often, Euka would bat at an unsuspecting errford and have two or more errford balls rolling around.

I could hear the errfords' joyous noises from where I was.

"I'm not complaining," I began, "but what are we doing here?"

Loher looked at me and smiled, "You're not used to not being in charge, are you?"

"Am I bossy?" I asked, genuinely curious.

"No," she laughed and gently kissed me, "you're a natural leader."

We stood there for a few moments, sharing my coffee, enjoying the sunshine and the warm tropical breeze.

An assortment of errfords had found their way aboard and were exploring everything they could see.

Loher gently took my hand and led me back to the mess hall to retrieve her own cup of coffee.

I decided a refill was in order since we were there.

Balt was already feasting on whatever Cook had thrown together for him, as the dwarf wasn't fussy.

The stench of old seafood was almost overpowering.

"Good morning, all," Captain Magnus sang as he entered the room and bypassed the coffee, "what are you eating, Balt?"

"Leftover squid," he swallowed, "an' some o' t'is cheese," Balt burped and continued to stuff his gob.

Chunks of squid and crumbs of cheese were mixed into his already filthy beard, adding to his, shall we say, charm.

A large chunk of cheese dropped from his beard and landed with a plop into Balt's mug of ale.

Captain Magnus suddenly looked ill as Cook attempted to hand him a plate of eggs and sausages, "On second thought," he dry heaved, shook his head, and left the room.

Balt belched again and watched the captain's retreat, "Musta been sumptin' 'e ate."

We excused ourselves, coffee in hand and cautiously followed the captain to see if he got sick.

Captain Magnus was found leaning half over the railing, sweating, and breathing a bit heavier than usual.

I chanced a peek over the side and saw millions of tiny fish, swirling violently in the water just below where the captain was leaning.

"Are you alright, Captain?" Loher soothed and gently placed her hand on his back.

Captain Magnus wiggled his head incoherently.

"Can you stand up?" she asked and attempted to help him to his feet.

"Did you see it?" Captain Magnus asked, regaining a bit of composure.

"See what?" I asked.

"Balt..." he moaned.

"In the mess hall?" Loher asked.

We were confused.

"That..." Captain Magnus dry heaved, "that chunk..." another heave, "ch-chunk of cheeeeese," he turned and vomited over the rail once again.

The sound was incredible.

Meeka quietly approached and whispered, "Is he drunk?"

"No," I whispered back.

"He's puking, right?" she asked, trying not to giggle.

"Twice I know of," I whispered.

"Do you know why?" she giggled.

I shrugged my shoulders, "Something about Balt and cheese, I don't know," I chuckled.

Meeka's smile widened as she fully began to giggle and shook her head in disbelief.

Loher looked in our direction, her hand still gently upon Captain Magnus's back.

It was more than obvious that she too was holding back uncomfortable laughter.

"Kuchoff?" Meeka asked as she finally walked up and tried to comfort him, "Are you alright?"

He regained his composure and looked at her with a weak smile.

"Did you drink too much last night?" Meeka giggled.

"No," he cleared his throat and spit something out over the railing, "I was fine this morning until I saw Balt in the mess hall."

"I hadn't the pleasure," Meeka commented.

Captain Magnus stared out into the vast sea, "He had this nasty looking chunk of cheese dangling from a squid tentacle," he lightly heaved again, "stuck in his beard. But then it fell off and went into his drink."

He dry-heaved again.

Meeka suddenly looked a bit squeamish herself, "I'm glad I didn't see it," she breathed.

"Me too," Loher agreed with a sour look on her face.

I took a sip of my coffee in hopes the bitterness would stop me from heaving.

"But that was only the start," the captain complained, "it was the smell that did me in," he laughed weakly.

"The smell?" the wizard giggled.

"Old squid, pungent cheese, stale ale and his normal bad breath was just enough to make me sick," he began, "Add that to a late night surrounded by eline warriors..." he stopped and thought, "You know they use that small tent just outside of the command tent as a...litter area?"

"I'm not quite following," I admitted.

"Their toilet," Captain Magnus breathed and scrunched up his face, entailing an overpowering odor.

"That bad, huh?" Meeka teased, giggling, "Did they make you use it?"

"Alright," Captain Magnus laughed, "I'm done with *this* conversation."

⚬

While Nitch went off to visit his tribe, Captain Magnus gathered everyone remaining into the command tent.

We were met by Cirdan and his team.

"I don't smell anything," Meeka whispered to Captain Magnus, making him snicker.

Cirdan looked around at the occupants of the tent and realized that there were unfamiliar faces among us.

We had a quick 'meet and greet' and even introduced Euka, who enjoyed being around so many other felines.

No one took her ability to speak as strange.

Navari, on the other paw-hand, was a different story.

Medusans were not known by these particular eline, so they had no latent fear of her.

They were, however, fascinated by the snakes growing out of her scalp.

"I have to admit that I was never expecting to see any of you again," Cirdan began, "but I am thrilled to be mistaken on this issue."

"I think most of us somehow *knew* we would make it back here," Captain Magnus replied raising agreements from most of the crew.

"And you're sure you can return back to your own realm?" an eline warrior asked from the mixed crowd.

Murmurs and soft discussion hissed throughout the tent.

"We are," Meeka confirmed.

More quiet discussion.

"Captain Magnus and I sat down last night and discussed the reason for this visit," Cirdan announced, hushing the crowd. "It seems those marauders that were attacking us last time are still at it and growing stronger."

Mentions of the Grand Ascendancy and hushed discussions swept across the tent once again.

Roars of reminisce of the battles fought echoed throughout the tent.

One could actually *feel* the excitement growing in the air.

"It gets better," Captain Magnus called over the crowd, "now's your chance, Balt."

Balt cleared his throat and simply growled, "T'ere be **dragons** ta kill."

Silence.

Balt chuckled, "T'eir all yers, Cap'n."

"What did we miss?" Nitch asked loudly as hundreds of errfords suddenly spilled into the tent.

Balt cleared his throat once more and uttered, **"Dragons."**

The tent suddenly began to glow blue as just the mere mention of the word, 'dragon' struck enough fear into the errfords, to form a collective bubble over the entire tent.

"Well," Captain Magnus laughed, "at least *that* has been confirmed.

After the errfords settled down, Cirdan continued, "We have been asked to return with them to Beornan Heafod to aid in the fight against the Grand Ascendancy."

"And dragons!" Balt added.

A collective cacophony of cheers, roars and excited chitters erupted, puffing the sides of the tent out a bit.

After all the noise had subsided, "Where are we going to live?" an eline voice called out, raising more discussion.

"Wherever you'd like," Meeka answered, "here, there, anywhere."

"Can we live in the Wudu?" another voice called out.

"If you'd like to," I answered.

"What about Larix?" he asked.

I stood and stared at him for a moment, trying to decide if he was being serious, or just trying to push the boundaries, "Do you *want* to live in Larix?" I asked.

He looked at me uncomfortably and then lowered his eyes, looked down and shook his head, 'no.'

"Can we join your King's army?" a female eline asked.

"Only if you swear your true allegiance to him and accept him as your King," I answered, "after that, then yes, yes you can."

"I am absolutely *positive* that he would *love* to have a unit of eline warriors," Meeka vouched, "Errfords as well."

"What about your crew?" another eline asked.

"I'm sorry," Captain Magnus stated, "what about my crew do you mean?"

"Can we join your crew?" the eline asked.

"If you are willing to accept me as your captain and leader above anyone else, besides the King and swear a blood oath on it, successfully learn how to work aboard a ship and poop like a human, then yes, you may join my crew."

A low roar of discussion and laughter filled the tent once again.

"A blood oath?" I whispered into Captain Magnus's ear, "Poop like a human??" I giggled.

Captain Magnus smiled, "Of course not," he quietly laughed, "but let's see if they're willing. I won't *make* them do it. The blood oath, I mean."

It was a good plan; I nodded in agreement.

"So, we can just mix into polite society?" Cirdan asked, trying to clear up any related questions.

"Absolutely," Roash purred, "we've been there, Rion and me," she stated, "and we've experienced the way goodish people will treat us and I can honestly say that it's not bad."

Rion agreed wholeheartedly.

"Take some time to think about it," Captain Magnus announced, "We're going to stay here for a while and recuperate."

"Think of this as a small vacation," Meeka giggled.

"Dismissed," Cirdan roared.

The eline warriors began to file out of the tent in an efficient, orderly fashion, while the crew of The Scorpion just kind of bumbled around in a confused manner creating a slight bit of chaos.

Captain Magnus looked embarrassed, "We're going to have to work on that."

"Give Commander Reetah two weeks, and they'll all fall in line," Cirdan boasted.

"Reetah?" Meeka asked, "Rion's sister?"

Cirdan was surprised that the wizard knew who she was, "The same," he answered.

"Is she willing?" Captain Magnus asked, intrigued.

"Eager, actually," Cirdan purred.

"There goes that small vacation," Meeka groaned.

⸺◆⸻

The first week of Reetah's training course went as badly as I had expected, but by the middle of the second week, she had everyone falling in line with the rest of the mixed crowd.

A few more days and we were ready.

The ground training was complete, and the sea training was about to begin, by walking The Scorpion onto the beach as a sort of dry dock so we could inspect the hull.

Minor repairs and a few upgrades later and she was ready, more than ever, to sail out and get into some trouble.

But first...the actual sea training, just like Captain Waxx had done with us.

What took my team and I almost a year to perfect, took less than two months for the eline to learn.

Not only were they skilled assassins and warriors, but they turned out to be fairly decent sailors as well.

If this race *had* been imbued with magic, they would undoubtedly be an unstoppable force.

We anchored for one last night on the island to conclude our small vacation.

<hr>

"All aboard that's coming aboard," a crew member called from the bow of the ship as the mixed crowd scuttled about, stowing gear, and choosing available bunks.

Everyone on the island was given the choice to either stay on the island or go on the presumably deadly mission to seek out and destroy the Grand Ascendancy and their dragons.

A small handful of crew members, mainly the older and injured, elected to stay behind, while the majority of eline and a sizable number of errfords chose to go with us to explore and fight.

Cirdan decided to stay behind.

I think it was because he was unwilling to give up his command and especially because he didn't want to be commanded.

One can only speculate.

With the final crew member aboard, The Scorpion pulled up anchor and began sailing in the direction of where we arrived.

We had discovered a pair of pointy rocks, the portal stones, just below the surface of the water when we were teaching the eline the ins and outs of sailing.

Meeka had a feeling the portal stones would be out there, close to where we appeared; she was right.

With the tome on the deck in front of her and the wand in her hand, we approached the portal stones.

"Eight meters," Captain Magnus called from the bridge.

Meeka made sure she was ready.

"Seven meters."

She closed her eyes.

"Six meters."

She took a deep breath.

"Five."

She thought about Avilyn Harbor and The Dragonfly.

The portal opened and we sailed straight in.

CHAPTER TEN

FULFILMENT

We emerged through the portal into darkness.

"I can't see a thing!" the helmsman cried.

"Port!" Meeka yelled, "Port!"

The helmsman quickly yanked and spun the wheel, making the ship lurch to the left.

As our eyes adjusted to sudden night skies, we recognized The Dead Dunelands uncomfortably close to the starboard side of the ship.

"That was close," Meeka breathed.

"Too close," I agreed.

A chorus of cheers and roars poured out from every corner of the ship as we turned toward Avilyn Harbor.

"May I?" Captain Magnus asked as he placed a hand on the ship's steering wheel.

The helmsman blinked in surprise and stepped aside, "She's your ship, Captain."

With Captain Magnus at the wheel, we bypassed Avilyn Harbor and sailed directly toward the Den.

The helmsman leaned against the wall of the bridge and produced a pipe, which he lit and drew a long pull, "You're not afraid, Sir?" he asked through a thick puff of sweet fragrant smoke.

"Of sailing at night?" Captain Magnus laughed, "No, were you once?"

The helmsman coughed and corrected, "Of the Grand Ascendancy, Sir, and dragons."

"Of course, I am," Captain Magnus admitted, "but I'm more afraid of what Amaliya is going to do if we don't stop her."

There was a long pause of silence until the helmsman asked, "Rumor has it that Amaliya is your birth mother, Sir, is it true?"

Captain Magnus laughed, "Who told you that?"

"It's just talk, Sir, don't let it bother you."

"It would only bother me if it *wasn't* true," Captain Magnus chuckled, "which is why *we* have to be the ones to stop her."

"I can honestly tell you, Sir, that I feel a whole lot better with more errfords aboard."

"What about the new eline warriors?" Captain Magnus asked and offered the wheel back to the helmsman.

"With all due respect, Sir," the helmsman began as he retook control of the ship, "eline are no different than dwarves in my book, glad to have them around in a battle, but underfoot the rest of the time, causing unneeded ruckus."

"So, you're not enjoying this?" Captain Magnus chuckled as he headed toward the door.

The helmsman smiled at his captain and said, "It's better than a sharp spear in the eye, Sir."

Captain Magnus laughed and began walking to the bow to find Meeka.

He found us, Loher included, lounging, and stargazing on the deck near the harpoon.

We were laughing and relieved that we had accomplished recruiting such a formidable fighting force.

The ship looked abandoned; other than the necessary crew on duty and small packs of errfords scuttling about, one would barely guess we had so many 'people' on board.

"The helmsman just asked me what I'm afraid of," Captain Magnus chuckled as he joined us down on the deck.

"What did you tell him?" Meeka asked.

Captain Magnus laughed and said, "I told him that I was afraid of the ship's hold becoming a litter box."

We all laughed.

"I'm teasing," Captain Magnus admitted, "I told him that I was afraid of what Amaliya is going to do if we don't stop her."

The mood went somber.

We sat in thoughtful silence for a few moments until Exland Mountain could finally be seen, looming over the port side of the ship.

"We'll be home in about an hour and twenty minutes," I claimed, "I'm going to go get my gear packed up."

"Good idea," Captain Magnus agreed as he youthfully sprung up from the deck while I creaked and groaned on my slow ascent to standing.

Meeka stood up with barely an issue, "there's this thing I've been doing that Roash showed me," she said as she twisted her body into an odd position, "it's called yoga, or something, you should try it."

Loher looked immediately interested, while I thought I'd give it a chance sometime in the future.

I smiled and excused myself down to our quarters to gather our gear.

Captain Magnus followed suit.

When I returned, Captain Magnus was still gone, but Roash and Lybi had arrived, adding to the ongoing conversation about hair care and whatever that yoga stuff is.

They all seemed interested.

I handed Loher her gear and began to head toward the starboard side of the ship, to disembark once we arrived.

The Scorpion crawled over the land barrier and gently settled into her lagoon bath, safe and sound in her den.

Everyone aboard, besides the necessary crew, disembarked into the hidden underground cave system.

The caverns and chasms echoed happily with the sound of life.

"It's a good thing you built all of those housing units throughout the Hollow," Lybiidae praised.

"We was expectin' t'is ta 'appen, Lass," Balt chuckled, "we planned fer it."

A small drey of about a dozen or so errfords suddenly scurried past us, investigating every nook and cranny they could fit their tiny hands into, chittering and balking at each other in their own natural language.

We continued our stroll.

Walking past my house, I could see that Loher was attempting to explain that yoga stuff to Navari, contorting herself into odd stances, trying to keep her balance; I found it the funniest when Navari shook her head in confusion, so they went inside.

"What do you think about Roash's yoga stuff?" I asked Navari.

"I be t'inkin' 'bout tryin' it," Balt said in all seriousness, "might 'elp me fight better," he stopped and looked at us, "Can't hurt, can it?"

"You're serious, aren't you?" I asked the dwarf.

"As serious as me axe blade's sharp, Mate."

"No Balt," Lybiidae commented, "it couldn't hurt."

"But me *blade* sure can!" the dwarf roared with laughter.

"You've got a good point, Balt," I shared, "Just look at Roash," I offered, "I've never seen anyone fight like that before, perhaps there *is* something to this yoga stuff."

"Her acrobatic skills far exceed even mine," Lybiidae complemented, "I'd *love* to learn how she does it."

"Could you imagine if Balt could flip around like that?" I chortled.

"Or Brot'er Fost," Balt howled.

"Don't be surprised when some day he does," Roash giggled from within the shadows, "I wasn't really spying," she said as she appeared into the light, "I was actually coming to join your stroll, but heard you talking about yoga and I wanted your honesty about it, so I hid," she confessed, "I'm sorry."

We all brushed it off as nothing and continued our stroll.

"You could really teach me how ta do jumpy spinny flips, Roash?" Balt excitedly asked after a silent moment.

"You won't be my first lumbering musclebound student."

"Rion?" I guessed.

"Both he and Cirdan," she laughed.

"Wow," Balt gleamed and strolled off on his own, dreaming of 'jumpy spin flips.'

"I'm sure he'll sleep well tonight," I laughed, "I'm hungry. Galley anyone?"

"I'm sure Cook will need help unpacking," Lybiidae acknowledged, "I'll join you."

"I wonder if he's got any more of that squid left," Roash purred.

My stomach did a 'jumpy spin flip.'

As with any pride of felines, it took a few weeks for a 'pecking order' to establish itself within the eline ranks.

Naturally, Roash, being the most experienced of the group, was selected as the Alpha, while Rion was chosen as the Beta.

The position of Gamma had violently switched paw-hands a few times until a young orange tabby male called Nixx could not be bested.

The errfords established Nitch as their immediate leader, as he was already an elder of the tribe.

Nitch's second was a female called Pok.

It took the errfords a while to pick their battle buddies, but we all eventually ended up with a compatible errford partner with more than a few dozen errfords to spare.

My errford battle buddy was called Nib.

A fearless female, she was smaller than most of the other errfords.

Did I happen to mention that errfords reproduce rapidly?

They do.

It also wasn't extraordinarily long until we had a few new eline cubblings scampering around the den as well.

"Do you ever think about settling down and starting a family?" I asked Loher as she gently cuddled an eline cubbling.

She looked up at me with a glow to her face, "Do you mean children?"

I blushed, "Not *exactly*," I chuckled, "do you *want* children?"

"Eventually," she smiled and returned her attention to the cubbling in her arms, "after Captain Magnus is safe and we can relax. These people are our family," She said, "we practically helped Meeka raise him."

"It looks like we're helping raise these little ones as well," I chuckled and gently scratched Loher's little friend behind the ear.

The cubbling began to purr and fall asleep.

Two sharp whistles suddenly screamed through the cavern.

"Enemy ship!" I gasped and began to sprint to the lagoon.

Loher smiled, handed the cubbling back to its mother and took off after me.

By the time we arrived at the lagoon, a mixed army was already boarding The Scorpion.

We had plenty of crew members to go around.

Enough for a fresh crew every time The Scorpion went out, with some left to spare.

The Den always had personnel residing within.

"How far away is it?" I asked as I entered the bridge.

"You can relax," Captain Magnus chuckled, "they're not coming this way," he said, "they've only been spotted but we *are* going after them."

"T'at's wot I wanna be hearin'," Balt growled and tapped the blade of his axe on his helmet, "I'm gonna see if anyone needs t'eir armor or weapons worked on." The dwarf hurried away, calling for dull weapons and damaged armor on his way.

Below deck, in the hold, Balt had set up a rough workshop in the cabin across from his own, including a proper fireplace/forge.

It was common to see random weapons and pieces of armor tossed on the floor just inside the workshop doorway; placed there for Balt to work on.

There was a similar, better workshop built into the Hollow as well.

I decided to see if he had any takers, so I went down, and wasn't disappointed.

A line of crew members, human and eline alike, had formed in the hallway and scattered into the hold.

Banging, pounding and a whole lot of cursing in Dwarven could be heard above the sound of the waves bashing against the hull.

I silently took my leave and returned to the upper deck to gauge our current situation.

Without a spyglass, I could see a dark speck on the southern horizon.

It looked to be heading southwest, toward the mainland south shore, past Bom'dabo.

"Are you sure it's them?" I asked Captain Magnus.

"Absolutely," he smiled and handed me the spyglass.

I raised the spyglass to my eye and had a closer look.

Surely enough, it was a dark ship flying the same purple flag as the last few ships we encountered and destroyed.

My heart skipped a beat as I scanned out in front of the ship and saw a dragon in the sky above them.

"Thare be a **dragon** out there, Captain!" I gasped, doing my best Balt impression.

Captain Magnus laughed in disbelief, "Stop fooling around."

"I'm *serious,* Sir," I breathed, handing the spyglass back to him, "look forward and above the ship."

He raised the spyglass to his eye and scanned the area then suddenly called out, "Helm, as the crow flies, with haste."

"Aye, Sir."

We turned directly toward the enemy ship and gave chase.

We closed the distance between the two ships quite quickly until the other ship, now identified as The Warlock, rounded the bend, and disappeared temporarily behind the tall trees of the forest surrounding the Seolfer Wudu.

As we rounded the bend, word of the dragon spread quickly through the ship and crew members were gathering in groups, trying to get a glimpse of it.

Nitch was already stationing his fellow errfords around the railings of the ship in case a shield was needed.

It was more than obvious at this time that the crew of The Warlock knew we were chasing them, as they decided to turn broadside and lob off a few rounds of cannon balls at us.

Our errford reinforcements guaranteed the cannon balls just bounced harmlessly into the sea.

The errfords then lobbed a few rounds of their own magical artillery back at them, causing The Warlock to tip violently to one side and begin to take on water.

The Warlock, now sitting lower in the water, righted itself, turned away from us, and continued their chase of the dragon.

We continued to gain on The Warlock, the distance closing fast, "Claws!" Captain Magnus called out with a toothy grin.

"Claws, aye, Sir," a voice called from below.

The Scorpion seemed to jump to life as we closed in on The Warlock and grabbed it with her claws, raising the ship out of the water and then fiercely slamming it back onto the water's surface, severely compromising the ship's structural integrity.

The Scorpion overtook The Warlock and continued to chase the dragon, leaving The Warlock to slowly sink beneath the sea.

"Amaliya?" Meeka asked.

"She wasn't aboard," Captain Magnus stated.

"How can you be so sure?" she asked.

"That was way too easy," he claimed, "had she been aboard, we would still be engaged in battle."

"That's a fair point," Meeka giggled.

"Now we git ta deal wit t'at beautiful beastie," Balt sighed, enamored of the flying reptile, "I can't wait ta kill it."

"Why are you so violent, Balt?" Meeka rhetorically asked, chuckling.

"Why ain't ye?" Balt retorted, seriously.

She just cutely batted her eyelashes at the dwarf, kissed Captain Magnus on the side of his head and slipped out of the bridge.

The Scorpion was gaining on the dragon, and we could clearly see that it was green, just like Kusagi, the young dragon we had killed in The Hollow so many years ago.

We were approaching the river that separates the Beornan Heafod mainland in half; the dragon began to fly closer to the shoreline, dipping lower as well.

"It looks like it will follow the river inland!" Navari called from the bow.

"We'd better catch it before it makes landfall and destroys a town," Meeka breathed at Captain Magnus as he walked up on us.

"Roash," Captain Magnus called, "do you think you can make that shot with the harpoon?"

She analyzed the distance between the harpoon and her target, "No," she answered, "we're not within range."

"We don't have enough line, or the physical distance is too great?" he asked.

"Not enough line," she answered.

Captain Magnus drew his katana and cut the line from the harpoon, "Don't miss," he warned, "I want my harpoon back."

She looked at him as if he had sprouted another head.

"Knock that flying lizard out of the sky," Captain Magnus ordered.

"With pleasure," the eline commander hissed through her sharp teeth and turned to the harpoon.

Roash took careful aim and squeezed the trigger.

The untethered harpoon sailed directly toward the dragon and found purchase exactly in the joint between the left wing and the breast.

The witnesses aboard all cheered as the dragon plummeted to the ground with a thunderous crash.

"That was a lucky shot," Roash breathed in relief.

"Lucky or not," Captain Magnus proudly began, "it worked. The dragon is down."

"It still be alive!" Balt cheered as a plume of dragon fire erupted from within the Charon Swamp.

"Get us closer!" Captain Magnus commanded.

"Getting closer, aye, Sir." The helm called back.

"She's coming toward us!" the crow's nest called down.

"Cannons!" Captain Magnus called out.

"Cannons ready, Captain," a voice called from below, "on your mark."

"Archers!" Loher called out.

Lybiidae and several crew members reported to the port side of the ship, bows and arrows at the ready.

Meeka had also arrived and began chanting an ancient spell.

Without warning, the dragon stampeded out of the swamp and breathed an enormous cloud of dragon fire at The Scorpion, drenching her in flames.

Her sails burned away, leaving her drifting, being pulled toward the river by the current.

Sadly, the crewman stationed in the crow's nest was cooked to a crisp.

"Fire everything we've got!" Captain Magnus commanded with a downward arc of his arm.

"Aim for the eyes!" Loher added.

A volley of virtually point-blank cannon balls, arrows and an over-sized ice ball impacted across the entirety of the dragon's face.

We were blind and deaf for a moment.

Thick smoke hung in the air, obscuring the view, our ears ringing from the blasts also made hearing anything difficult.

Another blast of dragon fire erupted, consuming the trees around the area.

"Cannons?!" Captain Magnus called.

"Cannons almost ready, Sir." The voice called from below.

"I really hate to tell you this, Captain," I began, "but the river is taking us in and away from the dragon."

"I need legs!" Captain Magnus called as he began to move toward the stairs to the hold.

"Legs," a voice called out, "aye, Sir."

"Belay that," Captain Magnus corrected as he bolted down the stairs, "I'm on it myself."

"As you wish, Captain."

Captain Magnus mounted the controls for The Scorpion's claws, tail and legs and the 'creature' sprang to life once again.

The giant scorpion found traction on the riverbed and crawled safely on shore.

"The dragon is a little to the left and forward about a half of a kilometer," I called from the bridge.

"A little port and forward," Captain Magnus echoed, "aye."

The Scorpion lunged forward, crawling across dry land and slowly began to veer left, toward her foe.

"I can see the dragon," Captain Magnus announced, "Have every-one report to either the cannon lines or their quarters until this is over. I also need a few errford volunteers to stand on the bow in case we need their shields."

"Aye, Captain," I replied and relayed the captain's orders to the rest of the crew.

More than half of the errfords volunteered for shield duty.

———————

The Scorpion slowly made her way toward the injured dragon.

The dragon was too busy trying to yank the harpoon from his broken wing to notice The Scorpion creeping up on him.

She circled around so she was coming up to the dragon from behind.

Slowly she crept as to make as little noise as possible, inching closer and closer.

Snap.

The Scorpion had stepped on an unseen branch or twig, alerting the dragon of her presence.

He spun around and breathed dragon fire across The Scorpion's upraised claws.

A bit too late, the errford shield suddenly made The Scorpion glow with a light blue aura, putting out the flames.

She brought one of her claws around and smashed the dragon across his snout.

The dragon winced in pain and drew his head back and away to avoid the second claw.

Whipping his tail around, the dragon attempted to smash The Scorpion across her starboard side.

His tail impacted with a jarring crunch, tossing everyone aboard about a meter to their left.

We regained our footing and began to shoot arrows at the beast.

Our arrows had no effect on the dragon's thick armored scales.

Errford orbs began pelting the dragon wherever they happened to land, creating slight pock marks across his scales.

The Scorpion drew closer to her foe.

Unable to breathe fire again so soon, the dragon swiped at The Scorpion with his tail once again, knocking her out of claw's reach, and then retreating into Charon Swamp.

The Scorpion unloaded her starboard cannons, but the dragon was moving fast and was already out of range.

The Scorpion followed him into the swamp.

His trail was easy to follow due to the blood pouring from the harpoon wound and a discarded, damaged dragon scale lying here and there.

We found him at the base of Monere Tower, still trying to remove the well-placed harpoon, but only creating a larger wound in the process.

In the places where the errford orbs had hit, some of the scales were either loose or already missing.

We fired our arrows into the places where his scales were missing, drawing blood with every impact, but doing insignificant damage.

In an attempt to evade The Scorpion, the dragon began to scale up the side of the tower.

We unloaded our port cannons, impacting every projectile across his back and tail.

The impact of the cannon blasts forced the dragon into the wall of the tower; bricks and mortar began to rain down in front of The Scorpion.

The dragon continued to climb, only to step on a loose portion of the damaged wall.

The wall caved in and sent the dragon falling toward us.

The dragon impacted the ground hard, knocking more bricks and debris down on top of him.

The Scorpion grabbed the fallen dragon by the wing and struck out with her tail, impacting the beast in the side with the missing scales.

Her 'stinger' found purchase within the leathery flesh of the injured dragon's ribcage, tearing out large chunks allowing the blood to flow.

"That *had* to have broken a few ribs," I thought aloud.

"The scales are thin enough to penetrate," Loher acknowledged, "once the errfords weakened them."

The dragon tried to breathe fire on us again, but it only came out as a spurt of flame that lasted less than a second, doing no damage at all.

Realizing his folly, the dragon yanked his broken wing back from The Scorpion and began to climb the tower once more.

With no other choice, The Scorpion began to attempt to climb up after him, using fallen rubble as steppingstones.

The combined weight of both the dragon and the massive, heavily armored ship, mixed with the age of the ancient tower was a recipe for disaster.

Huge chunks of the tower began to crumble away until the whole structure completely collapsed on top of the pair of combatants, burying them both beneath tons of rubble.

The entire tower had finally fallen.

⸺ ◆ ⸺

A soft hacking sound could be heard from beneath the rubble, and then the sound of laughter.

"'Ere's yer damn harpoon... Sir," Balt said sarcastically as he handed the blood covered harpoon back to his captain.

"Now we just have to dig our way out of here," Captain Magnus chuckled and dusted himself off.

"I feel bad about destroying this beautiful, old tower," Lybiidae sighed.

Balt broke out into uncontrollable laughter; Captain Magnus began laughing as well.

"What's so funny?" the Drow elf asked.

"Ke.." Balt tried to speak but couldn't due to laughing so hard.

"What?" she asked.

"Kennis..." Balt laughed.

"And Shannon," Captain Magnus gagged out through chuckles.

"Who are Kennis and Shannon?" she asked.

"We had met them while trying to save Thunor's life," Captain Magnus breathed, trying to calm down.

"T'ey wanted us ta destroy t'is tower..." Balt chortled.

"Back when I was about nine or ten years old!" Captain Magnus snorted.

Lybiidae began to giggle, "Mission accomplished."

"We should get back aboard so we can dig our way out of here," Captain Magnus suggested.

"Aye, Cap'n," Balt saluted sarcastically and followed his companions aboard.

⸺◆⸺

Using the natural abilities of a real, live scorpion, she used her eight legs and tail as shovels and easily dug her way free, leaving the corpse of the dragon buried under the rubble of the fallen tower.

Crew members were sweeping and tossing debris over the side of the ship as we physically walked The Scorpion back to where we came out of the water.

"With almost everything above our heads burned away or broken," Captain Magnus announced to the crew, "we should be able to drift our way down the river, under the bridge and all the way to Salvus Hus for repairs."

Three cheers rose up from the ranks as The Scorpion rested back into the river and let the current take her to salvation.

CHAPTER ELEVEN
MONTHS LATER

Word of the battle between The Scorpion and the dragon spread throughout the realm like wildfire, adding to the mystique and legend of the famous ship, captain, and crew.

Teams of adventurers set out to explore the ruins of Monere Tower; some returning with odd trinkets of treasure, some never to be seen again.

With new grey sails and reinforced rigging, to a brand-new coat of black paint and everything in between, including iron armored claws, The Scorpion was reborn and better than ever.

We were moored in the common docks of Avilyn Harbor, stowing provisions, recruiting new crew members, and dismissing those who chose to leave the crew.

Many of Captain Waxx's older crew members retired from The Scorpion, either to settle down, or join a safer, less ambitious crew.

It was known throughout the realm that The Scorpion was embarking on a dangerous and suicidal mission to search out and destroy the Grand Ascendancy, along with any other dragons encountered on the way.

Most of the residents of the realm were in favor of the mission, due to the destruction the Grand Ascendancy has caused, including the re-introduction of dragons into this peaceful realm.

People of all races and origins gathered around the docks to have a chance to see the famous Scorpion up close.

Once known as a dreaded and feared pirate ship, now seen in a new light as a sort of hero ship; a redeeming feature, if you will.

The line of potential new recruits was endless, so we could be choosy about who we allowed to join and who we turned away.

Only a small number of eline decided to go off and explore their new realm, while every errford decided to remain aboard.

A few more than a dozen elves, Drow included, decided to join the crew both out of curiosity as well as honor for Loher and Lybiidae; and a bit for me, I guess, as I am half elven.

Balt ended up recruiting two more dwarves and a few large men for away missions in particular.

Tybidon Trislee was among that group.

Captain Magnus decided to take him on with reduced rank, as an ensign, due to his experience aboard The Dragonfly.

He was not bad in battle either.

"Didn't I tell ja Mon, dat royal banner wouldn't be lastin' too long," a familiar voice announced from the dock below.

Captain Magnus's face began to glow with his ever so goofy, toothy grin, "Captain Waxx?" He guessed correctly as he turned and looked over the railing.

"It just be Mario now, Mon" he called up, "permission to come aboard, Captain?"

"Granted!" Captain Magnus beamed and ran for the gang plank stopping only to tell a passing crewwoman to have Commander Ashpin report to the bridge immediately.

"De Scorpion be lookin' good, Kid," Mario commented as he reached out for the young man's hand.

Captain Magnus bypassed the old pirate's hand and dove in for a hug, "I've missed you," he admitted.

Mario embraced the young captain, "Been thinkin' 'bout 'cha too, Mon," he sniffed.

Captain Magnus gently pulled away and smiled, "I know someone else that would love to see you," he sang and gestured the way to the bridge, "lead the way."

"Bridge?"

"Aye, Sir." Kuchoff chuckled.

Meeka was just arriving at the bridge as the two men walked up, "I didn't see anyone in there, so I thought she was joke...*Captain Waxx!*" she screamed and threw herself into his arms, almost knocking him through the doorway.

They stood in an embrace for a moment until Mario cleared his throat and gently patted Meeka on the back.

She pulled away and wiped tears from her cheeks, smiling at the older man, "You're not thinking of rejoining the crew, are you?"

Mario laughed, "No, not me," he paused, "My son, Tatenda," he explained, "I waited until he was signed onto de roster before I let ja know I be here, Ma'am."

"You *do* understand that we're actively going after the Grand Ascendancy, right?" Captain Magnus warned.

"It's going to be dangerous," Meeka added, "are you sure?"

"It's not up to me, Mon," Mario replied, "Tatenda wants to serve aboard De Scorpion *because* of de mission."

"Is he good with a blade or bow?" Meeka asked, "Or magic?"

"Better," Mario smiled, "he helped design and build de original 'Creature' device and knows tricks wit' 'er even *I* don't know." Mario looked at Meeka, "Proficient wit a blade, better wit de bow an' I don't understand magic, but he can use it advantageously."

"If you were his captain," Captain Magnus began, "what rank would you give him?"

"Lieutenant Commander," Mario answered without hesitation.

"Done." Captain Magnus stated, "I'm sure Lieutenant Commander McLaaud has met him and knows his qualifications already."

"Speaking of which," Meeka sighed, "I should probably go back to my duties before they back up on me," she pouted with a giggle.

Mario gave her another hug and walked her to the door, "I'll leave ja to yer duties as well, Captain."

"Just don't be a stranger," Captain Magnus said with a salute, "Sir."

Mario smiled, saluted back, and disappeared through the doorway.

⸻ ⬥ ⸻

"What have they done to you?" Tatenda rhetorically asked as he inspected the creature controls.

He set down his pack, opened it and dug around for a moment, producing an odd-looking set of tools.

He selected a tool and mounted the controls, wrenching away on them, cursing in Drow the whole time.

Two errfords began to rummage around the contents of Tatenda's pack, chittering out of curiosity.

"Can you give me a hand with this?" he asked, "Grab that long skinny tool and look for a hole by my left foot."

One of the errfords handed me the proper tool and I located the hole.

"Stick the pointy end into the hole and twist it to the right until it stops," he instructed, "and then keep twisting even harder until you're sure it won't twist anymore."

I complied and twisted the tool for a few seconds until it stopped and then twisted with more strength, "Done," I advised.

"Thanks, now step back," he gestured.

I tossed the tool back to the errford, took a few steps back and watched as he pressed down on the left pedal.

There was an extremely loud grinding sound as the whole ship suddenly lurched forward and settled into a different standing position.

"I think perhaps we should move away from the harbor before you fix this any further," Captain Magnus suggested with a nervous chuckle.

"Aye, Captain," Tatenda smiled and walked The Scorpion out into the Strait of Avilyn until her legs couldn't reach bottom.

He then pressed down on both pedals and the legs folded up, setting the ship down easily into the water; we were now floating.

The Scorpion swished her tail and began to move in a forward direction, as if swimming, although real live scorpions cannot swim.

Alternating his foot pedals, The Scorpion began to kick her legs and started to turn around.

"I guess there's no real need for a helmsman anymore is there?" I chuckled.

"Yes, there is, Sir," Tatenda stated, completely missing my admittedly poor joke, "we would travel much too slowly like this."

Captain Magnus and I smiled at each other, noting the kid's naivete.

The Scorpion reached the southern shore of the Dead Dunelands and began to crawl at a moderate speed onto dry land.

Within moments, The Scorpion was treading through the sand.

"Let me show you what this baby can *really* do, Sirs," Tatenda requested.

"The controls are yours, Lieutenant Commander," Captain Magnus granted.

Tatenda pulled a lever and announced, "Attention all crew," he began, his voice somehow echoing throughout the ship, "creature operations will commence in a moment. Please secure yourselves."

He waited for a moment, counting the seconds in his head until he reached a certain number and then began to pedal, pull, and twist at the controls.

The Scorpion sprang to life and began running across the desert, as if she had been moving in sand the entire time.

She located a dead, fallen tree and picked it up with her claws, and began wielding it like a club.

She swung the tree at another, standing tree and knocked it out of the ground, landing it a few dozen meters away from where it once stood.

She dropped the tree and began to walk toward the mountains.

After a few hundred meters, she suddenly veered off to the left toward a burned-out ancient dragon skull.

When she got within striking range, she thrashed her tail forward and smashed the skull into large chunks and then turned back toward the mountains.

Upon reaching the mountains, without hesitation, she climbed up the side of the mountain and rested at the peak.

The view was spectacular to say the very least.

The castle at Salvus Hus could barely be seen from this height and distance but was indeed visible to the naked eye.

With a good spyglass, virtually the entire realm could be seen from here.

"I can see my house from here," a crew member chuckled and pointed in the general direction of Powell raising even more laughter from the crew members standing around him.

Captain Magnus quickly sketched out a rough map of what he could see and then returned to the hold, "Take us back down, Lieutenant Commander," he ordered, "we're heading back to the Den."

"Returning us back to the water, Sir," Tatenda replied and began to guide The Scorpion down the mountain toward the sea.

"Impressive controlling, Tatenda," Captain Magnus complemented with a gentle slug to the shoulder.

"Thank you, Sir," he smiled and continued to rest the giant scorpion back into the sea.

"Helm," Captain Magnus called as he bound back up the stairs, "Den please."

"Going home, aye, Captain."

The sails were raised, and The Scorpion began to cruise back to her aquatic cave.

Once we arrived at The Scorpion's Den, Tatenda crawled The Scorpion back into the lagoon, "Will I be needed for a while, Sir?" he asked me as I began walking toward the stairs.

"I'm sure we're in for the time being," I answered, "and you don't have to 'sir' me," I added, "we're the same rank. My name is Thunor, or McLaaud, whichever."

"Thank you," he smiled, "Thunor," he closed his eyes while still mounting the creature controls and quickly fell asleep.

He looked peaceful, so I didn't bother him with the fact that he had his own quarters in The Hollow.

I began to walk to my own quarters, carefully stepping over errfords scampering around the hallway of the hold.

I accidentally kicked one, and a light blue ball went rolling down the hallway, bouncing off the walls and doorways.

"I didn't kick you *that* hard," I chuckled as the errford screamed in delight, rolling along, seemingly able to control the direction of movement.

"I've got our things ready to disembark," Loher informed me as I entered our quarters.

"That was something else, wasn't it?" I commented about Tatenda's creature controlling.

"It's almost as if he were practiced at it," Loher smiled, oblivious about who was at the controls.

"He is," I chuckled, "that was Tatenda Waxx, Mario's son."

She looked up at me with a surprised look on her face, "He's on the crew?"

"We just recruited him today," I answered, "according to Meeka, Tatenda actually helped design and build the original controls."

"Makes sense," she smiled, "so that's his station?" she asked hopefully.

"It is," I answered, "no one better for the job. He's asleep at the controls as we speak."

"That's dedication," Loher laughed and handed me my gear, "I'm tired as well, I think I'll sleep tonight, let's go."

"Trislee joined as well," I mentioned.

"I have no problem with the commander," she commented as we disembarked.

"Ensign," I corrected, "Captain Magnus recruited him as an ensign."

"Why the demotion?" she asked as we walked toward our house.

We paused for a moment to allow a group of a dozen or so errfords to cross the walkway in front of us.

They continued exploring, and climbing on everything they encountered.

"They're all so *cute*," Loher gushed at the mass of errfords.

"Captain Rina suggested it due to his immaturity at times," I answered and opened our front door.

"Suggested what?" Loher asked, distracted by the cuteness overload.

"Ensign Trislee's demotion," I chuckled.

"She knows him best," Loher chuckled and closed the door behind her, tossed her gear in the corner and headed straight to bed.

I wasn't far behind her.

Chapter Twelve

GROUNDED

I awoke to the sound of rolling thunder and gnashing waves.

Loher was still sleeping peacefully beside me.

I kissed her gently on her head and got out of bed.

Quietly, as not to wake her up, I donned my gear and slipped out the front door.

Somehow, a handful of errfords had gotten into our house overnight because there were errfords sleeping almost everywhere I looked.

A nice cup of hot coffee from the galley was first on my agenda, so I made my way through the residential area of the Den and followed the welcome fragrance of fresh brewed coffee.

The galley was already serving a few eline and human crewmates while errfords were gathered around a large bowl of something they were enjoying.

Lybiidae, helping in the galley, handed me a cup of coffee and offered a chunk of bread, which I refused.

She smiled and bid me good morning.

Moments later, 'activity potion' in hand, I arrived at the lagoon to watch the storm.

The Scorpion was safe and secure in her lagoon and barely anyone else was up and around.

A bright bolt of lightning lit up the entrance to the Den followed closely by the crash of expected thunder.

I smiled at the spectacle and took a cautioned sip of the steaming hot beverage.

It was warm as it ran down the back of my throat, the aroma invaded my nostrils sending sensations of smokey, rich goodness throughout my entire being.

Another lightning flash and its companion, thunder.

"It be comin' down in sheets, eh McLaaud?" Balt half whispered behind me to not startle me out of my thoughts.

"I've always loved thunderstorms," I breathed in awe at the next flash of lightning.

"Eh," Balt grunted, "t'ey ain't bad."

His words were enhanced by the rolling thunder that followed the flash.

"You can relax, gentlemen," Captain Magnus announced as he stepped into view aboard the ship, "with this storm, we're not going anywhere."

"Who be stressin'?" Balt sarcastically called back to him.

Captain Magnus smiled and disembarked to dry land below.

"I was, a little bit," I quietly admitted and took a sip of coffee.

Balt grunted out a chuckle and began to walk to meet the captain.

"But don't think we have the day off," Captain Magnus advised, "Roash has a little training for those interested."

"Flippy spinnys?" Balt asked with excitement.

"The same," Captain Magnus smiled.

"Ooh when?" the dwarf asked, "Where?" He began frantically looking around for Roash.

"Take ease my eager friend," Captain Magnus laughed, placing a hand on the dwarf's shoulder, "she won't be starting for a few hours, but if you want to find her, I suggest you start by the dry pantry. She and Navari are hunting for their breakfasts."

Lightning flash...

Balt shuddered, "Live rodentia," he moaned and placed a hand on his belly.

"I wonder how the errfords feel about that," I wondered aloud.

"Good question," Captain Magnus agreed and thought about it for a few seconds.

Rolling thunder...

"I'm gonna go find Rion," Balt coughed impatiently and began to walk away.

"He's probably there with them," Captain Magnus teased.

"Dammit," Balt cursed and continued to walk away with his head hung low, pouting in a way.

"Hey, Balt," Trislee called from the galley doorway, "let's munch something."

"Now yer talkin'!" Balt smiled and headed for the door.

Lightning lit up the cavern, the wind blowing rain in, creating a light mist.

I rolled my eyes and laughed.

A crack of loud thunder followed by more lightning...

"It certainly doesn't take much to keep him happy, does it?" Captain Magnus rhetorically commented.

A whipcrack-like thunderclap seared our eardrums, undoubtedly waking everyone within The Hollow.

A small group of errfords scattered into glowing blue streaks, rolling quickly across the floor in all directions.

I had no intention of laughing, but the sight was just a bit too much and I burst out in laughter.

The storm was intensifying and the waves just outside of the hidden cove grew large enough to spill into the lagoon within.

"Hurricane?" I guessed.

"Monsoon, Sir," a crew member corrected as he passed by on his way to the galley.

"We're not going *anywhere* in *this*," Captain Magnus repeated and gestured to the galley.

"Remember that chunk of cheese?" I giggled.

"Ugh," Captain Magnus frowned sourly, "thanks for reminding me, let's wait."

I smiled and nodded in agreement.

The two new dwarves Balt had recruited ambled past us and into the galley, acknowledging us as they passed.

"That clinches it," Captain Magnus laughed, "I'm suddenly not hungry anymore."

I noticed that my cup was void of coffee, "Are you going to the galley?" I asked a passing crew member.

"Aye, Sir," he replied.

"Would you mind returning this for me?" I asked.

"It's not a problem, Sir," he answered and took the cup.

"Thanks," I smiled, "enjoy..." I called to him as he entered the galley.

Captain Magnus chuckled and began to walk toward the ship.

"Besides Roash's training," I began, following him to the ship, "what else do we have in store for us today?"

"First off," he said, patting his growling stomach, "I'm going to find some breakfast. I'm sure Cook has *something* stashed aboard."

"I should have kept my cup," I laughed and followed the captain into the ship's mess hall, "Then what?" I asked as I started making fresh coffee.

"I don't know," he murmured as he shuffled through the pantry, "it depends on this storm."

He emerged from the pantry with his famous toothy grin, holding up two large strips of dried meat.

I offered him a cup of coffee and exchanged it for a strip of meat.

The storm raged on, rocking the ship gently in her lagoon as we sat and shared our meal.

Periodically, an errford or two would scamper through the room, picking up the odd morsel of food from the floor and either devouring it on the spot, or stuffing it into a pouch, or a cheek for safe keeping.

"This storm kind of reminds me of when we ended up in Errford-land," Captain Magnus shuddered.

"You don't think this storm is caused by..." I began but Captain Magnus smiled and shook his head before I could finish my question.

"No," he half chuckled, "that storm was somehow...different," he said, staring off at the wall, unblinking, "Unnatural."

Meeka suddenly appeared in the doorway, finding us sitting on the floor, "I found them," she called out to the hallway.

Moments later, Loher appeared behind the wizard, "What are you two doing on the floor?" she laughed.

"Hiding from a piece of cheese," Captain Magnus burped.

Meeka giggled.

We offered the rest of our meat and coffee to them, but Loher refused and helped me to my feet instead.

"I gather we're grounded," Meeka commented as she poured herself a cup.

"We are until this storm passes," Captain Magnus replied, chewing.

"Roash has that stretching flipping training thing today," I offered.

Loher's eyes lit up, "When does that start?" she asked excitedly.

"Who do you think is more excited," Captain Magnus asked, "Loher or Balt?"

"Balt, by a long shot," I laughed.

"Come on, Loher," Meeka scowled at us playfully, "let's go find Roash."

The wizard grabbed the rogue's hand, and the pair of women exited the ship in willing search of impending torture.

We decided to follow them out of sheer curiosity.

⁌⚬⁍

Roash decided that the floors of the Den and Hollow alike were too uneven, so she held her training aboard The Scorpion.

Surprisingly, the deck in question was almost full of willing participants including all three dwarves, every single eline on the crew, a handful of elves, a whole bunch of humans including Ensign Trislee, and quite a few errfords.

"I almost feel like I should join in," I nervously chuckled.

"Me too," Captain Magnus admitted.

"Lead by example?" I suggested.

Captain Magnus pondered this in his head for a moment and then agreed, "It couldn't hurt, could it?"

We snuck into the crowd just moments before Roash began to speak.

"If you're just here to learn how to do the flips and jumps," she began, "you're in the wrong place," she looked at the vast majority of the crowd as they began to disperse, "*but...* if you start here and now," a mixed portion of the crowd stalled and waited for her to continue, "in time and with disciplined dedication, you will find that you can, indeed, jump and flip and spin."

More than half of her potential students left the deck, leaving Loher, Lybiidae, Euka and Meeka, all the eline, the errfords that were already present, Balt and his two friends, Ensign Trislee, four other hulking men and a handful of women, both human and elf.

"Okay then," Roash continued, "more of you stayed than I expected." She admitted with a smile.

A wave of chuckles and giggles ebbed through the crowd.

"Yoga is about breathing and stretching," she began, "it's not about fighting or killing, although it sure helps."

The eline in the room collectively grunted in agreement while Balt snorted out a chuckle.

She continued explaining the history and benefits of the art form and then paired all the non-eline students with an eline partner of equivalent size and build.

The three dwarves were paired with younger, shorter eline, which was beneficial to both races.

The errfords paired off amongst themselves.

Roash started us off slowly for the first few days as the storm continued over the realm, but after a straight six days of training, most of us began to pray for the storm to finally pass.

———◆———

"I'm not sure how much more of this training I can stand," Captain Magnus laughed and stretched over his cup of coffee, "I'm sore all over."

"Who said, *'It couldn't hurt, could it?'*" I mocked his words from a week before, teasing.

Captain Magnus laughed and groaned, "Can *you* jump any higher yet?"

I laughed and shook my head.

"Disciplined dedication," Captain Magnus grunted as he slowly stood up, "let's go check on that storm, it seemed to be letting up a few hours ago."

"Aye, Captain," I groaned as I attempted to get up from the floor.

"Come on, old man," Captain Magnus teased as he helped me up with a slight grunt of his own.

The Scorpion was sitting still in the water as we entered the bridge and looked through the mouth of the Den.

The weather was cloudy and hazy, but the sea was as calm as before the storm and it wasn't raining any more.

"How long until daybreak?" Captain Magnus asked the helmsman.

"About an hour, Sir," he answered, "Are we departing?"

"Without a doubt, Lieutenant," Captain Magnus smiled, "without a doubt."

"Aye, Sir, I'll begin to rouse the crew," he informed and left the bridge.

Captain Magnus and I went off in separate directions to spread the news.

❧

An hour or so later, The Scorpion was out in open water, on the hunt for the Grand Ascendancy.

We decided to circle around Haze Mountain, in hopes of quickly finding them and stopping them once and for all.

Chapter Thirteen

THE DRAGON AND THE HOOD

Haze Mountain loomed large up ahead.

Commander Ashpin had her tomes and wand ready in case we needed to chase them through a portal and was already standing up front on the bow.

"We're not going to be there for another hour and a half or so," Loher mentioned as she observed the wizard getting prepared.

"I'm not taking any chances this time," Commander Ashpin vowed.

"Look," Navari hissed and handed Loher the spyglass, "is that what I *think* it is?"

Loher peered through the spyglass and scanned the area around Haze Mountain, "Is that...*red?*"

"Is *what* red?" I asked, my heart jumping like a jackrabbit.

Loher looked horrified as she handed me the spyglass.

I raised the spyglass to my eye, hands unsteady and scanned the mountaintop, "*Captain,*" I called, "you may want to come take a look at this."

Commander Ashpin snatched the spyglass from my grasp and quickly looked.

She too looked horrified as she handed Captain Magnus the glass.

"Another dragon?" Captain Magnus guessed as he looked, "Oh wow," he said calmly, "it's red."

"Is that all you're going to say? 'It's *red*'... really Kuchoff?" the commander asked, surprised at his calm reaction.

"Before any of you ask, yes, I know the difference between the different colors of dragons," Captain Magnus stammered, "Red is really no different from green, only they're a bit tougher and their fire breath is acidic as well."

"If it bleeds," Nixx, the eline Third, stated from directly behind me, "it dies."

"Where did you come from?" I asked, slightly startled by his sudden appearance.

"I've been standing here the whole time, Sir," Nixx answered.

"Well, now I feel bad that I didn't acknowledge you," I admitted.

Nixx roared in laughter, "I jest, Sir," he chuckled, "I only just arrived when you had the glass."

Loher and Commander Ashpin giggled, in on the joke.

"I'm glad everyone finds it so easy to play and joke around while there's a *red dragon* flying around out there," I stated, "And if we can see *it*, it can *easily* see us."

"Fair point," Captain Magnus agreed, "Spread out and *calmly* warn everyone. We don't want to cause any panic from the new recruits."

"I'm going to stay here and keep focused," Commander Ashpin stated.

Captain Magnus nodded his agreement and rushed off to warn the others.

Within minutes, hundreds of errfords began to line the rails of the entire ship, some had actually made nests and stations on the railing itself.

They were ready to spring the shields whether we needed them or not.

Quite a few have already begun shielding themselves, along with portions of the ship.

Eline warriors began to mingle about the upper deck, eager to see their new foe, while Balt and the dwarves settled into the mess hall for their pre-battle feast.

Cook was not enthusiastic.

We were getting closer to the mountain and by this time the dragon had definitely spotted us as it was flying a figure eight around us and the mountain top.

The dragon was enormous, twice, maybe three times bigger than the one we last slew.

Roash had positioned herself at the harpoon, line still cut from the last time.

Four more new harpoons sat on the deck near her feet, Nixx ready to load the next.

"Circle around to the portal stones but stay around ten meters away and hold position," Captain Magnus ordered.

The helmsman complied and The Scorpion began to circle around to the north side of the island.

Captain Magnus turned and asked me, "Do I need to ask, or is Tatenda already on the controls?"

"He's already there, Sir," I smiled, "awaiting your orders."

Captain Magnus smiled and kept his eye on the dragon, "I've got a feeling we're going to need him."

⸺⸺◆⸺⸺

The Scorpion had crawled up onto dry land and positioned herself on the southeastern edge of the Dead Dunelands, hiding in plain sight.

Haze mountain was three kilometers due south of her position.

If the Grand Ascendancy or anything else emerges through the portal, The Scorpion could quickly intercept without warning.

We sat and waited.

Hours passed as the weather became clearer and clearer.

The dragon flew off in the direction of the mainland and disappeared within the peaks of the Ferrum Mons.

Balt was a bit unnerved for a moment until the dragon ascended above the mountain tops and began to make its way back toward us.

Soaring high above Avilyn Harbor, it suddenly swooped down at a tremendous speed.

We began to think it was going to dive right into the sea, but at what seemed like the very last moment, the dragon skimmed the surface of the water and seized a giant fish with its talon-like feet.

It then swooped up and perched atop the highest peak of Haze Mountain and began to eat.

We sat and watched this rarely seen gift of nature, barely noticing the movement to our right.

Hushed calls of another dragon spread quickly around the ship as an iridescent dragon five times the size of the red dragon came soaring into view from somewhere near Avilyn Harbor.

We looked on in awe as the larger dragon ascended above the clouds and disappeared.

"If I didn't know any better," I breathed to whoever could hear me, "I'd swear that was Avilyn."

"The elf?" Loher questioned.

"No," I chuckled, "The King of all dragons," I answered, "*That* Avilyn."

"How would you know what he looked like?" she asked, still scanning the sky.

"Do you remember what Kuchoff looked like when we killed that first dragon," I asked, "about twenty years ago?"

"Kusagi," she remembered, "Kuchoff..." she paused in thought, "Yes! I *do* remember."

The red dragon, enjoying its meal, was caught off guard as the iridescent dragon suddenly appeared, hovering over the mountain, descended and flew directly into him, knocking the pair of dragons over the side of the mountain and into the sea.

"Go, go go!" Captain Magnus ordered, pointing at the brawl.

"Spitting image," Loher agreed after catching another glimpse of the dragon.

The Scorpion stood up from her resting spot and quickly crawled into the water.

Her sails puffed out and she began to cautiously sail toward the fighting dragons to get a better look.

The dragons were thrashing around in the shallow water on the northeastern end of the island.

Although the red dragon was the smaller of the two, it had somehow managed to pin the larger dragon to the rocky shoreline, breathing acidic fire into its face.

"Harpoon!" Captain Magnus called.

"Which one?" Roash called back.

"Both!" Captain Magnus answered with a shrug of his shoulders.

"Aye," Roash purred and took aim at the red dragon.

She squeezed the trigger and sent the first harpoon straight into the back of the red dragon's skull.

The acidic fire suddenly stopped, giving the injured dragon a chance to retaliate.

A thick cone of frost erupted from the iridescent dragon's gaping maw and froze the red dragon solid.

"It's *pink* now," Commander Ashpin uncontrollably squealed in delight and awe.

The surviving dragon clawed at its frozen foe and shattered the corpse into chunks that quickly floated out to sea.

"Ready harpoon," Captain Magnus commanded.

"Already done, Sir," Nixx advised.

The dragon looked directly at The Scorpion, raised its wing as if to shield itself from any potential projectiles, and began to strafe away.

"Hold," Captain Magnus calmly said and placed his hand on Roash's shoulder.

She took her finger off the trigger and relaxed her arm but never stopped aiming at the dragon.

The giant dragon suddenly spread its wings and jumped into the air.

Ascending quickly, it circled around the ship twice and then slowly began flying toward the portal stones.

"Shall we follow it, Captain?" the helmsman asked.

"With haste," the captain answered.

"Aye."

We followed the dragon as it rounded the bend and began to slowly descend toward the portal stones.

The portal flashed a mere second before the dragon disappeared through it.

I counted only seven seconds before we entered the portal behind it.

*

"Where are we?" I asked, my eyes scanning the sky for the dragon, but finding nothing due to the tall trees surrounding us.

"I wasn't thinking of anywhere," Commander Ashpin stated, "I didn't even have my wand out."

The tome was laying open but face down by the wizard's feet.

She bent down and picked it up to see what the map looked like, but the book suddenly slammed shut, pinching her finger, and losing the page.

She looked up at us with a confused and worried look on her face.

"Let's try and make the best of the situation," I soothed, "just look around, it's *beautiful!*"

We were sailing through a gentle river, just large enough to accommodate a large ship, such as The Scorpion.

The land was green and thick with foliage, most of which were tall pine trees.

The air was warm and smelled fresher and cleaner than I was used to.

The sun was bright overhead and streamed through the canopy, creating odd shadows and bright spots.

It was unlike anything I had ever seen.

Birdsongs of many varied species filled the canopy above us as we slowly drifted peacefully down the river.

"Full stop," Captain Magnus breathed as he surveyed his surroundings.

"Full stop, aye, Sir," Helm replied.

I felt a tug on my arm from below, "I made a note where the stones are, Sir," a voice announced.

I looked down and saw one of Balt's dwarven friends holding a crude map up to me.

I smiled and took the map, unsure of what to do with it as this was usually Brother Fost's position, "Thank you, ...umm..." I had no idea what his name was.

"Rhodi," he offered, "My name is Rhodi, Sir, I'm Balt's brother."

"And the other dwarf you're with?" I asked out of curiosity.

"Ridi, Sir," Rhodi answered, "we're all brothers. You can tell by our names."

"How so?" I asked, not even trying to hide my ignorance.

"Our names, Sir," he repeated, trying to think of a way for me to understand.

"Me *real* name be Cobalt Copperbottom," Balt explained, strolling into the conversation, "T'is be me big brot'er, Rhodium Copperbottom an' our baby brot'er Iridium, but we call 'im Ridi, is in t'e mess hall schoolin' Cook a t'ing 'r four about dwarven cookin'."

Captain Magnus's stomach did a flippy spin.

I handed Captain Magnus Rhodi's map, "Rhodi sketched where the stones are," I informed.

"Most appreciated," Captain Magnus smiled and slugged the dwarf moderately in the shoulder.

Rhodi smiled and snuck off to the mess hall.

"Okay team," Captain Magnus called as he pointed at his senior officers, "we need a vote," he looked at his closest friends...family, "Do we want to turn around and go back, disembark and explore, or stay aboard and follow this river? Discuss."

Roash began, "Personally, I'd like to get out and explore on foot and I'm sure there are more eline than myself that feel this way."

"We could follow the ground team with the ship at the same time," Commander Ashpin added.

"Two teams," Balt suggested, "one on eit'er side o' t'e ship an' a ..." he stopped and thought for a moment, "'Ow many 'Poofers' do we gots?"

"Poofers?" Captain Magnus asked, sustaining a chuckle.

"Like Meeka," Balt pointed at the wizard, "poofy smokey magic stuff." He explained waving his hands in the air.

"He means my 'blink' spell," Commander Ashpin guessed.

Balt continued to point at the wizard, waving his finger in her face, "Yeah, *t'at's it!*"

"Besides me," Commander Ashpin pondered, "I think two others, elves, can cast 'blink' or something similar."

"I never learned that one," Loher admitted, "it would've come in handy in my thieving days."

"Doubtful," Commander Ashpin countered, "It usually has to be line of sight unless you're absolutely sure of your surroundings, or you've left a token." She suddenly frowned, "I watched a young wizard blink right into a tree."

"Did he die?" I asked, afraid of the answer.

"Not right away," she grimaced, "he struggled to free himself, screaming in pain the entire time until Master Ficolus put him out of his misery."

Balt giggled something about Cirdan and then tried to look serious.

"Do you know which elves, Commander Ashpin?" Captain Magnus asked.

"I think so," she answered, "Loher, why don't you come with me," she said, dropping a coin on the deck, "we'll track them down."

Loher smiled and followed Commander Ashpin to find the elves.

"So, what's your plan, Master Dwarf?" Captain Magnus asked after the two disappeared down the stairs.

"Shouldn't we wait 'til Meeka an' Loher git back wit' t'e elves?" Balt asked.

Four women suddenly appeared out of three separate plumes of smoke, "We tried to hurry," Commander Ashpin smiled and picked up her coin.

"Your plan, Master Dwarf?" the captain repeated with a chuckle.

"Wot was t'e coin fer?" the dwarf asked.

"It was my token for blinking back," the wizard explained, "This blink wasn't line of sight, so, as I explained before, I needed a token. The coin."

Loher smiled, turned to her right and blinked forward about twelve meters, no smoke.

"No smoke?" she frowned.

"You *blinked!*" I exclaimed.

"I did, didn't I?" she beamed and gleefully ran back to me, "You're a great teacher, Meeka!"

"Just be *careful*," Commander Ashpin pled and looked at Loher with pride.

Captain Magnus cleared his throat and smiled at Balt, "Your plan?"

"Ow many people can ye poof?" Balt generally asked.

A discussion began between Commander Ashpin and the two elves, excluding Loher, as she wasn't quite experienced enough yet.

A rough estimate was guessed as about a dozen people per magic user.

"Two of ya stays aboard t'e ship for emergency poof backs an' two of ye poof a team each ta each side o' t'e ship an' explore. T'e Scorpion'll follow along all slow like."

There was a bit of discussion about his plan and after a moment, "Who will lead each team?" Roash asked.

"You lead the portside team and Balt will lead the starboard team," Captain Magnus decided.

"Can I 'ave Rion?" Balt asked.

"He's yours," Roash gifted, you can have Trislee as well."

"T'ank ye muchly," Balt smiled.

"I'll be staying aboard, just in case," Captain Magnus added.

"In case of what?" I asked.

Captain Magnus smiled shyly and shrugged his shoulders, "Captain's prerogative," he smiled, "Commanders, pick your teams. Dismissed."

"We be *commanders* now?" Balt chortled and began to search for his preferred team members.

⸺ ✦ ⸺

The Scorpion slowly crept along the river, keeping an eye on her crew ashore.

An army of dozens of eline warriors, elves and humans scattered around the shorelines, searching for any sort of sign or clue as to where we were.

Hours went by with no added information or challenges, besides the odd shallow area on which The Scorpion had to crawl to get to deep water again.

No signs of non-animal life could be found until Ensign Trislee came across a faint trail leading off into the forest.

Humanoid footprints were found on the trail, but Navari's thermal vision picked up no traces of heat, proving the tracks were old.

"Roash," Captain Magnus began, "take a team and follow that trail for a few kilometers. If you don't find anything within a reasonable amount of time, come back and we'll continue down the river."

Roash nodded and gathered a team of dark colored eline warriors, each with an errford tucked safely within their armor.

"And don't engage anything unless you absolutely need to," Captain Magnus added as the team began to leave.

They virtually disappeared before they even left the shoreline.

Approximately an hour later, the team reappeared from the trail.

"Fifteen men, armed with simple looking blades and bows, about four kilometers up the path, Sir," Rion reported.

"Hostile?" Captain Magnus asked.

"Potentially, but doubtful, Captain," Roash replied.

"Why doubtful?"

"They're laughing, playing some sort of game or competition," she stated, "or so it looked to me."

"All human?" Captain Magnus asked.

Roash nodded affirmation.

Captain Magnus glanced around at his crew, "Trislee and McLaaud, you're with me. McLaaud, hide your ears, Commander Ashpin, the ship is yours."

Nitch jumped onto Tybidon's shoulder while I felt my own volunteer errford crawl between my chest and plate.

Within a moment, I must have gotten used to her being there, because I couldn't feel her anymore.

A few seconds later, we emerged on shore within a cloud of pink smoke.

"Lead the way, Ranger," Captain Magnus gestured to me.

I began down the trail, keeping an eye out for footprints and other tracks.

Plenty of markings could be identified, including white tailed deer, timber and grey wolves, and fox, among others.

Human footprints could be made out under the animal tracks informing me that this trail had not been used for quite some time.

The sounds of laughter and a slight odor of alcohol could be detected just up the hill.

Sounds of bowstrings snapping, arrows hitting their marks and men cheering erupted as we drew closer.

We cautiously crested the hill and saw the fifteen men, indeed having an archery competition.

We were noticed at once and met with friendly words and kind gestures.

"I am Robin," the apparent leader, a tall man in a green and brown hooded tunic announced with an obnoxious bow, "and this is my band of merry men."

The men looked rough and unkempt.

They were all young and looked frail, all but one, an exceptionally large, bearded man called John who carried an equally large wooden quarterstaff.

"I am Captain Magnus," Kuchoff bowed in respect, "And two of my men, Lieutenant Commander McLaaud and Ensign Trislee."

"A *captain*?" Robin flamboyantly asked, "of a ship or an army?" he teased.

"Both," Trislee spoke out of turn.

A few of Robin's men laughed.

"We're all gentlemen here," Robin laughed and bowed in our general direction, waving his hands in a grand gesture, "Have you an archer amongst your ranks?"

I silently stepped forward and produced my bow, wishing it was Loher's bow of accuracy.

"Excellent," Robin commented, "shall we?" he gestured to the target.

I climbed the rest of the way up the hill and stood amongst Robin's men.

"Be my guest," Robin offered with a swoosh of his hand.

I drew an arrow and notched it to my bowstring.

The men around me fell silent.

Pulling back on the bowstring, I carefully took aim at the center of the target, let out my breath and released the string.

My arrow flew true and sunk deep into the bull's eye of the target, sending shouts of praise into the air.

Bags of coins were wagered and chants of, 'split the wand' began to circulate.

"Split the wand?" I asked.

Murmurs and soft discussion of confusion rippled throughout Robin's men.

"Splitting the wand is when an archer splits the other archer's arrow on the target," one of Robin's men, a young man called Scarlett informed.

Robin notched an arrow to his bowstring and the men once again, fell silent.

Virtually without even aiming, Robin loosed his arrow, sending it rapidly downrange with a splintering thud.

Upon inspection, his arrow had indeed split my arrow in half; piercing the exact same space my arrow had pierced.

Robin's men suddenly erupted with pride and praise, some commiserating for me.

Unwilling to be bested by a complete stranger, I notched another arrow to my string, took aim and let it loose.

My arrow, as if by magic, split Robin's arrow in two, creating a sort of wooden star in the center of the target.

Ensign Trislee was the only one celebrating as the rest of us were shocked that I had pulled it off.

"I've never been bested by *anyone,*" Robin gaped. "I must have your name once again, Good Sir."

"McLaaud," I answered, "Thunor McLaaud."

He shook my hand and tried to give me a large bag of coins.

I refused and charged him to give it to the needy.

He accepted and gave the bag to a drunken Friar named Tuck for safe keeping.

We sat and enjoyed each other's company for a moment.

They had no information about the Grand Ascendancy and we even got a chuckle out of them when we asked about dragons.

Obviously, they hadn't seen one nor do I think they believe that dragons even exist.

We bid them farewell and returned to the ship.

Meeka blinked us back aboard and we reported our findings.

"Well," Captain Magnus sighed, "I'm sure we're wasting our time in this realm, let's turn around and take our chances with the portal stones."

"Aye Captain, returning course," Helm answered, "Creature, about face," Helm called.

"About face, aye," Tatenda called from below, and The Scorpion stood up and turned around in the narrow waterway.

She sat herself down and began to traverse the river, back to the portal stones.

Errfords began to station themselves about the railings around the ship.

"Seven meters," Commander Ashpin called to the helm and produced her wand, thinking about Avilyn Harbor.

Her tome began to tremble, and at the five meter mark, it flipped into the air and landed on the deck, open to the map of Beornan Heafod.

CHAPTER FOURTEEN

SCORPION VS. VIPER

The portal flashed and we found ourselves sailing quickly toward a large dark ship full of hobgoblins and orcs.

It was flying the odd purple flag of the Grand Ascendancy.

Amaliya was aboard, standing on the bow.

Without warning, as if they were waiting there for us, they let loose a volley of cannon fire directly at our bow.

The Scorpion's claws deflected most of the projectiles, but a few came through and smashed into the lower portion of the armored bow.

There was little to no damage.

Repair crews were immediately dispatched.

Without hesitation, or even a *chance* to correct her course, The Scorpion slammed into the Grand Ascendancy's ship, The Viper.

The force of the impact shoved the two ships toward the southern shore of the Dead Dunelands, scraping the bottom of The Viper on the shallowing sea floor.

Unable to move and portside cannons exhausted for the moment, The Viper just sat there, helpless.

The Scorpion quickly snatched The Viper within her claws and raised it out of the sea.

She began to crawl out of the water, but The Viper's crew had reloaded their cannons and let loose another volley.

Without the safety of her armored claws, The Scorpion took the full brunt of the cannon fire into her face.

Cannon balls splintered through the railing, sending shards of wood and lead everywhere.

Luckily, Commander Ashpin had retreated to the hold during the first volley.

No one was injured.

Errfords by the hundreds bravely flooded the upper deck, casting their shields as they gathered.

The Scorpion began to glow within the safety of the errford bubble.

Another repair team was already patching up the damage to her bow.

The Scorpion, still gripping The Viper, stowed her sails, crawled onto shore, and smashed The Viper against a giant rock and into the sand.

Without letting go of her prey, she sprung her tail forward and struck The Viper on its port side.

A gaping hole was smashed into the side of the enemy ship, spilling cargo and heavy cannons into the desert below.

The Scorpion gave the ship one last shake and tossed it to the side like an old wine bottle.

Hundreds of heavily armed hobgoblins, orcs and human men began pouring out of the beached ship and began to rush toward The Scorpion.

With no orders given, the eline army disembarked The Scorpion and engaged the enemy in a land battle.

A clash of metal on metal, flesh and fur commenced sending roars and battle cries echoing throughout the Dunelands.

The blue glow of errford shields suddenly began to form around the individual warriors as they engaged.

"Request permissions ta join t'e battle, Sir," Balt asked.

"Granted," Captain Magnus smiled and drew his katana, "where are your brothers?"

"Waitin' wit Trislee by t'e plank," Balt grunted as we ran toward it.

Loher, Lybiidae and a band of elves intercepted us on our way, joining our group.

We each had an errford bodyguard by the time we reached the sand below.

Navari, a few elves, and a large group of errfords were already healing the wounded and sending the eager to fight directly back into the fray.

As soon as Captain Magnus and his team were clear of The Scorpion, she strode out onto the battlefield, stepping on marauders and swiping large groups of incoming enemy troops aside with her tail, killing many with each swipe.

Impossibly, thousands more enemy marauders continued to pour out of the damaged Viper.

The Scorpion grabbed the tree it had once used as a club and attacked The Viper, smashing it to bits, sending marauders flying into the air in every direction.

Amaliya and Lemac were suddenly exposed.

"We need better ships," Amaliya cursed as she and Lemac began to run for cover.

"Look, there," Lemac pointed to a huge dragon skull half buried in the sand, "we can hide there!"

"*We?*" Amaliya Magnus breathed in disgust, "*You're* going to get *your* ass out there and bring me back my prize," she screamed at him in anger, "*Alive.*"

"You're a *fool* if you think *I'm* going out there with all of those cat things everywhere," Lemac argued defiantly.

Amaliya clapped her hands together once.

Lemac suddenly dropped to his knees, cradling his head in his hands, screaming out in pain.

She stepped closer to him and held her lips millimeters away from his ear, "You *will* go out there and do as I command," she cooed.

She released her Psi grip on him and he fell to the floor in a weak lump of pain at her feet.

He weakly nodded his head in obedience and slowly stood.

"Now, *go.*" She commanded, pointing out from within the giant skull.

Black smoke began to rise around him as he puffed away and vanished.

❦

"I *saw* my mother on that ship," Captain Magnus called as we ran toward the wreckage.

"Are you sure she wasn't projecting again?" I called, jogging along with him.

"I'm positive," he breathed, slowing down a bit, "I can still *feel* her calling to me."

The enemy soldiers ahead of us were gathering as we ran toward them.

Friendly arrows cleared a path for us from behind.

"Did you Psi my second arrow?" I asked as I cut the legs out from under an orc marauder.

"What?" Captain Magnus laughed as he wiped blood from his legendary blade and prepared for another incoming orc.

"Did you help my arrow split Robin's wand?" I repeated, easily lopping the head from the shoulders of a passing hobgoblin, "Where was *he* going?" I laughed as the beheaded hobgoblin kept running for a few meters until he fell to the ground.

"Honestly," Captain Magnus called over his shoulder as he engaged a human warrior in mele, "I didn't even think to cheat."

"So that was all me?" I proudly asked as I witnessed his katana skills best his opponent after a moment of fighting.

Another orc sprinted away from the group running at the eline forces and tried to tackle Captain Magnus, but I sliced him in the kneecap with my eline blade and watched him fall.

He rolled toward the captain and tried to stand up, but Captain Magnus quickly impaled the orc, pinning him to the bodies beneath him with the orc's own pike.

We stood waiting for a few more marauders to arrive.

"I swear, I had nothing to do with it," Captain Magnus finally said, "So it must've been all you."

Commander Ashpin, Loher, Lybiidae and Euka finally joined us at our position.

Commander Ashpin began lobbing ice balls into the fray, knocking marauders either dead or unconscious, "If anyone gets thirsty..." she rhetorically sang, "I've got some nice, cold *ice balls* for ya!"

She pinged an ice ball into the side of a man's head and caved it in like a rotting pumpkin.

The human soldiers around him scattered in fright and panic.

"Nice shot," Lybiidae half giggled, half gagged.

"I love the way humans scatter like roaches with the first hint of danger," Roash purred as she arrived already covered in blood.

Captain Magnus cleared his throat in mock protest.

"Present company and crew excluded, Captain, Commander," Roash qualified, nodding at each respectively, "and you're half elf, McLaaud, so you were naturally excluded from the 'human' equation."

"Naturally," I chuckled as I thwipped an arrow into the eye socket of a charging hobgoblin.

"I'm digging a hole, aren't I?" she asked.

"Well, it *is* how you poo..." Captain Magnus began, but his laughter got the best of him.

A moment later, we were caught up in the fray.

"Here we go!" Roash roared and began slashing away at her victims with her iron claws, drawing blood and gore with every swipe.

Captain Magnus, Commander Ashpin and Euka all but disappeared into the fray, their blue errford shields glowing, still visible within the crowd.

Looking around, hundreds of blue glows could be seen in groups within the battlefield.

Loher and Lybiidae continued to pick enemies off, one by one from their vantage point high above, on the top of a dune.

"Save some for me!" I screamed as I drew my sword again and strategically entered the clash.

"Wee!" my errford companion, Nib, sang with glee as she cast her shield around us.

An immediate blade bounced harmlessly from my chest as I thrust my own sword into the chest of its owner, a large hobgoblin about the size of Rion.

It toppled to my feet, and I continued hacking and slashing at the enemy.

I swung my blade at a human and struck it in the back of his arm, severing it at the elbow joint.

He screamed out in pain, gripping his stump where his arm used to be.

Ensign Trislee suddenly rushed upon him, swung his Mourning Starr, and struck the foe in the center of his back.

Tybidon's deadly mass of lead and iron ripped completely through the body and sprayed blood and gore all over me.

Chunks of human rained down around us as Tybidon smiled with wild, crazy eyes as he ran toward the next closest foe.

A bit of the gore entered my mouth and the taste clicked something in my soul as my muscles began to throb.

Trislee swung his Mourning Starr at another enemy, a hobgoblin, striking it in its chest.

Again, the Mourning Starr never slowed down on its way through the hulking beast spraying a dark red mist, covering everyone in its wake.

Another blade ricocheted off my protected arm with no damage done, "I could get used to this," I chuckled to Nib as I blocked a hobgoblin's blade and stabbed in for the kill.

"Well, don't," she sneezed, "I may run out of energy soon. I'm not used to this, yet."

"I understand," I commented as I cut through another human marauder, "I'll just 'vamp out' as the captain likes to say."

"*You're* the vampire?" Nib breathed and tossed a human finger she had just bitten off to the ground.

"I *was* a vampire," I replied and yanked my blade from yet another marauder's corpse, "I retained some of the powers though."

"I'm interested in seeing that!" she giggled and expelled a natural orb at an advancing orc, impacting it directly in the chest, blowing a hole clean through it, *and* the next two marauders behind it.

Nib giggled at her triple kill.

I was about to advance on a large human male, but someone's arrow found its target in the back of the man's neck; the arrow protruding through his throat as he died and fell before me.

I had no time to call out my thanks, as another marauder began to pound on me with a war hammer.

Our errford shield took the hits as I turned around and grasped the beast by the throat.

"Now's your chance," I calmly growled at Nib and flashed my fangs at my prey.

The ogre I had in my grasp began to try to wiggle out of my grip, so I squeezed tighter, cutting off his airflow.

An orc tried to circle around me and stab me from behind, but I turned and blocked its blade with the ogre as a shield.

Two more marauders tried to pile on me, pouncing on me all at once.

They succeeded in knocking me down the pile of corpses I was teetering on to begin with, and then proceeded to roll over me, trying to smother me.

Nib's shield suddenly dropped, and I began to feel the weight of the two creatures atop me.

"I'm sorry," Nib whimpered and crawled away to a safer place within my armor.

My vampire strength wasn't enough to lift them off.

I decided to remain calm and think about the situation, but then I felt a jagged, probably rusty, blade enter my right thigh and twist.

Pain, unlike anything I had ever felt before, engulfed my thigh, and shot through my leg down to the ankle.

A sudden burst of strength erupted from my muscles, and I began to stand up, lifting the pair of marauders along with me: all on one leg.

Using the dead ogre as a crutch of sorts, I blindly slashed out with my sword and felt it impact on several objects around me.

I finally pushed the remaining load away from my face and realized I was surrounded.

Orc, human and hobgoblin marauders had formed a circle around me, yet no one was attacking.

I quickly stood up, relying on my good leg.

"Who stabbed him?" a large hobgoblin asked, pointing at the pooling blood by my foot.

His Common tongue had little hint of a hobgoblin accent.

No one admitted to stabbing me.

The hobgoblin grunted and then said, "Probably one of those corpses. He's no good to me *injured*," he spat.

I felt Nib move under my cloak, moving swiftly toward my wound.

A moment later, the pain went away and I regained feeling in my leg.

I decided to continue to lean on the dead ogre so the marauders didn't realize I had been healed.

My heart was racing and my muscles were twitching as I ran my tongue across my fangs.

"What *exactly* do you want with me?" I asked with a gurgling growl in my voice.

"We've never fought a vampire before," he commented, "we *all* want a go at you," he splayed his hand in an arc, gesturing at the army surrounding me.

Roars and laughs erupted around me.

I suddenly felt a bit more confident as a faint blue glow began to envelop me.

I smiled and slowly began to laugh along with them.

One by one, they discontinued their laughter as they each discovered me laughing along.

"What do you know of vampires?" I howled and fingered the pummel of my sword beneath my cloak.

"They only come out at night!" a human called out.

"And yet," I growled, "here I am, in daylight."

"They drink blood!" another voice shouted.

"And it looks like there's *plenty* to go around!" I snarled and licked my chops.

"They're hard to kill," the hobgoblin leader stated.

"*Wrong,*" I screeched and flashed to him with lightning speed and began to rip out his throat with my fangs.

The blood was thick and tasted metallic and sour as I drained the beast of his life.

I dropped the corpse and wiped my mouth with my sleeve, "We're *impossible* to kill."

The circle of marauders suddenly began to scatter in every direction out of fear and panic.

"I thought you all wanted a go at me!" I shouted at the fleeing masses, laughing.

"We *do,*" a deep voice growled behind me.

I spun around and saw two giant, well-armed (and armored) orcs standing before me.

"How do we begin?" I asked with a lick of my fangs, "one at a time or both at once?"

The orcs shot each other a panicked look.

"I'll decide," I said and stepped menacingly toward them in hopes of scaring them off, which didn't work, but I continued anyway, "Both at once."

I drew both blades and ran at them, preparing for the impact.

My sword impacted the orc on the right, but the orc on the left was no longer there.

The orc I had hit took no sustainable damage and tried to grab my arm but missed.

I slid to a stop in the sand and spun around to attack again.

I looked past my foe and witnessed Roash tangling with the second orc, trying to keep it from engaging me.

Off in the distance, I could hear dwarven battle cries and eline roars getting closer.

I engaged my enemy before he had a chance to react, as my actions only took a second or two to execute due to my vampiric speed.

I landed a solid blow with the flat side of my sword across his piglike face, playing with him.

He swung his crude blade in my direction, but I was already standing behind him.

Nib was thoroughly enjoying herself as we sped around the orc, making it angry and dizzy.

The more the orc failed to make any contact with me, the angrier he got and the more he swung at me, the dizzier and slower he became.

He was losing energy.

"I yield," the orc puffed, short of breath.

He dropped his weapon and stooped down with his hand on his knees, breathing hard.

Roash had dispatched her foe and was slowly walking up to us.

"He gave up," I chuckled as she arrived.

"I see that," she smiled and stared at the orc, "what you going to do with him?"

"I've already fed, so I'm not hungry enough to *eat* him…" I growled and wiped drying blood from my chin, "and I can't just *kill* him like this, can I?" I asked.

"I'm afraid that would be unethical," Roash purred.

"What would *you* do in my situation, my orcish opponent?" I growled, trying to enunciate my words clearly.

The orc looked up at me, smiled and said, "I wouldn't have stopped fighting, had *you* tired out. I would have killed you where you stood."

"Would you enjoy another go at me?" I asked, still trying to speak clearly.

The orc didn't answer.

Instead, he quickly lunged at me with both hands and grabbed me by the throat.

I started to laugh in his face, which angered him, and he began to squeeze.

He picked me up by my neck, so my feet left the ground.

I laughed even harder, which made him violently shake me like a ragdoll.

I looked directly into his eyes and saw a kindness there that I had never seen in anyone before.

I stopped laughing and purposely went limp as if I had died.

The orc stopped shaking me and held me out at arm's length, studying me to see if I was dead.

"Impossible to kill, my *hole*," the orc laughed and tossed me to the ground.

Roash was stunned and didn't move.

The orc turned to her, "*Your turn,* Puppet," he sneered and stepped toward her.

She adopted a defensive stance and prepared for the attack.

I sprang from the ground, surprised that my assault on his inner kindness worked and grabbed his head with both arms and twisted until I felt a sharp snap.

The dead orc dropped at Roash's feet.

"I *almost* thought you were really dead," she smiled and thanked me before running back into the fray.

I scanned the battlefield and noticed the number of living combatants was steadily shrinking.

The groups of blue were gaining in size.

"Ow many ya kill, McLaaud?" Balt asked as he and his two brothers climbed over a pile of the dead.

"I didn't keep track," I admitted as my fangs began to shrink back into my gums and I started to feel a bit more...elven.

"Thirty," Nib answered, "forty-three if you include *my* kills."

"Well done, Wee Lass," Balt complemented with a grin.

"I found this for your collection," she said and tossed him a jeweled ring, "sorry about the blood."

"No worries," Balt laughed and spat on the ring, he then wiped it with a dirty rag and held the ring to the sun, "Guid as new," he chuckled and dropped the ring into his purse with a wink at the errford on my shoulder.

"I gots twenty-six meself," the dwarf boasted.

"Thirteen for me," Ridi grunted.

"Fifty-one," Rhodi boasted.

An arrow came zipping about a half meter from my ear and impacted into a rushing orc I had my eye on.

"Thank you!" I called out.

"Welcome," Lybiidae called back from somewhere above and behind me.

After scanning the shrinking battlefield, I caught a glimpse of Roash and a few other eline assassins in their element, doing jumpy flips and spinny jumps, hacking, scratching and biting their victims, many of which never saw their killers before they died.

Rion was seen approaching our position, eating something he had in his paw-hand, "Why aren't you out there having fun?" he asked and took another bite of whatever he had.

"We be lookin' fer t'e captain an' Commander Ashpin," Balt excused, "What 'cha eatin'?"

He held the 'food' out for all to see, "I think it's a hand," he burped and took another bite.

It was indeed a hobgoblin hand.

"There he is," I pointed toward the wreckage of The Viper.

Captain Magnus was engaged in a sword battle with Lemac, a mixed crowd of both Scorpion crew members and Viper marauders circled around them, allowing for an uninterrupted, fair fight, almost like the one I just encountered.

We quickly made our way to the ring.

◆

With each strike, their blades rang out, singing a duet about the love of battle and death.

"If you kill me," Captain Magnus smiled with his usual toothy grin, "my mother will have your head on a platter. Literally."

Lemac thought about the captain's words and backed his fight off a bit, but only for a moment, "I do have to admit," Lemac replied, blocking a strike from Captain Magnus's katana, "it seems I may be in a losing battle."

Captain Magnus laughed, "No matter *what* you do," he lunged at the wizard again, "you're a dead man."

Loher shot an arrow through the neck of an orc that decided to bum rush Captain Magnus from behind.

The orc dropped at Captain Magnus's feet.

Angered, Captain Magnus took a deep breath, aimed his blade, and swung hard.

Lemac blocked his lunge and punched Captain Magnus in the jaw, knocking the captain unsteadily on his feet.

Dazed, Captain Magnus swiped again at his foe but missed.

Lemac punched him again, knocking Captain Magnus into the sand, his katana landing a meter away.

Rion and Roash began to charge into the ring, but Captain Magnus raised his hand, commanding them to stand down.

They complied as Captain Magnus rose to his feet and retrieved his weapon.

Lemac stood ready, allowing the reset.

Blood was oozing from the left corner of Captain Magnus's mouth as he spat blood into the sand and stepped closer to the wizard.

The wizard casually waved his hand at the sand beneath Captain Magnus's feet, moving the portion he was standing on out from under his foot, causing the captain to fall once again.

Angered, Captain Magnus got up, initiated a Psi-fist, and slammed it into Lemac, hurling him up into the air and sending him back a few meters.

Lemac landed on his head and fell unconscious.

"I tried to make it fair," Captain Magnus said to the sleeping man as he got up and dusted himself off, "but *you* brought magic into it..." he shrugged and walked away, "Bind him and put him in the brig."

"Aye, Sir," Ensign Trislee complied, smiling.

Nitch crawled out of his hiding place within Captain Magnus's armor and healed the captain's injured jaw.

"No shield?" Captain Magnus asked, rubbing his jaw.

"That would have been unfair, Sir," the errford countered with a slight chuckle.

"But that *hurt*," he laughed, still nursing his jaw.

CHAPTER FIFTEEN

AMALIYA AND THE SKULL

E uka suddenly ran up to us, "Amaliya has been spotted, Captain," she hissed, "hiding in a dragon skull just over there," she turned and stepped in the direction she was indicating.

"Does she know she's been located?" Captain Magnus asked and slowly began walking toward the skull.

"Unknown," Euka answered, "but I'm guessing she has no idea because she's still in there."

"Loher, McLaaud, Lybiidae, cloak and follow me," he ordered and began walking directly toward the skull, not even trying to conceal himself, "Roash, Rion, Navari and Balt, you're with me also."

The team complied and began to stroll toward the skull.

Psi bolts began to launch at us from within the skull.

Her aim was off as her bolts impacted nowhere near any of the team.

"Warning shots?" Balt asked as he quickened his pace to keep up with the captain.

"Probably," Captain Magnus laughed and held up a hand, "Steady," he called out to the team.

Loher and I kept to the tracks the team left behind, to conceal our own prints as Lybiidae, wearing boots of calm, left no tracks at all, and was free to find the best vantage point to help protect the team.

Once we arrived, Loher and I aimed our arrows directly at Amaliya from outside the skull.

We didn't want to risk being sensed or detected by entering.

Lybiidae was somewhere nearby, probably doing the same.

Balt, Rion, and Navari stood by with weapons in hand, while Roash and Captain Magnus stood just outside of the giant skull and tried to coax the enemy leader out.

"We know you're in there," Captain Magnus called into the skull, "We have Lemac in custody. You've lost."

No reply, just the sound of her shifting around on the sand covered bone.

"I can *see* you," Roash roared, her voice echoing through the skull.

"You're surrounded," Captain Magnus half lied, "there's no use in hiding like a coward."

He barely completed his sentence when we all suddenly flew back a few meters and landed in the sand behind where we were once standing.

The air temporarily knocked out of him, struggling to breathe from the Psi impact his mother just threw at us, Captain Magnus immediately got up and invoked a Psi orb in the direction of the skull.

The orb impacted the skull with a splitting crunch, shattering the ancient skull into hundreds of smaller pieces, once again, exposing Amaliya to the team.

She had a hopeless look on her face as she looked franticly for a place to run.

"Loher," Captain Magnus whispered.

"I'm right here," Loher whispered from somewhere behind him.

"She's got an old tin locket," he whispered to her, "find it and take it from her."

"My pleasure," the elven thief chuckled in a whisper.

Amaliya was desperately looking for cover as we all rose to our feet and began to advance on her position.

She turned and began to run until something stopped her and she fell to the ground with a violent thud.

I aimed my arrow at her, less than a half meter away.

Point blank.

Rion suddenly broke ranks and pounced on her, wrapping his jaws around her throat, biting down just enough to dent the skin.

Amaliya froze in place.

"Rion!" Captain Magnus snapped, "at ease!"

Rion loosened his grip and looked up at the captain but didn't move.

"Stand down, Rion," Captain Magnus barked, "That's an order!"

Rion dropped his prey on the ground and backed away.

She quickly stood up and dusted herself off with a disgusted look on her aging face.

"Hold," Captain Magnus commanded, and we all stopped where we stood.

Amaliya smiled and waved her hand as if to conjure some sort of Psi skill, but nothing happened.

We just felt a slight nudge that made us each correct our foot placement.

She looked horrified and patted at a pocket in her robe.

Loher suddenly appeared in front of her, holding up the locket and then handed it to Captain Magnus.

Amaliya scowled at them, showing her teeth.

"Navari," Captain Magnus laughed, "I think Mommy needs a nap."

Navari slowly strode toward Amaliya and dropped her hood.

Amaliya shrieked in horror as she recognized Navari's species and backed away blindly into Rion's arms.

Rion gladly gripped her by the arms from behind and forced Amaliya to look forward as the Medusan's eyes turned violet, "Sleep," Navari commanded.

Rion easily took the weight as Amaliya's legs dropped out from underneath her.

Amaliya was finally asleep and in Rion's custody as he cradled her like a child.

"Bind her and put her in the brig under constant observation," Captain Magnus ordered.

"Aye," Rion purred and carried his captive back to The Scorpion.

Lybiidae and I uncloaked and returned our arrows to our quivers.

"My brother, T'ferrow can put them into a temporary sleep stasis until we get to wherever we're going," Lybiidae announced.

Captain Magnus immediately answered, pointing at Lybiidae, "Do it."

Commander Ashpin stripped Lemac and Amaliya of any magical materials and objects before they were locked up securely and separately.

T'ferrow cast a dark sleep spell over them, proving escape to be impossible.

Navari and a few armed guards stood posted keeping a constant eye on the prisoners as we sailed to Salvus Hus.

"I thought you said you were going to kill her," Commander Ashpin reminded the captain.

Captain Magnus groaned and shook his head, "Don't remind me," he sighed, "as much as I want to, I'm sure she has valuable information, so she's worth more to us alive...for now."

"Navari could drag the information out of her," the commander stated.

"That's my plan for when we get to the castle," Captain Magnus frowned, "it almost seems like you *want* me to kill her."

"I think she's too perfidious to be allowed to escape," she qualified, "she'll use her Psi skills as soon as she has the slightest of chances."

"Not without this," he finally smiled, dug around in his pocket, and produced the locket.

Commander Ashpin took the locket and asked, "What *is* this?"

"Open it," Captain Magnus whispered, "carefully."

She pried off the cover of the locket and slowly opened it.

The locket contained a lock of hair, a few fingernail shards, and a few human baby teeth.

"They're mine," Captain Magnus said, "without them, her Psi skills are weak at best."

"Are you serious?" Commander Ashpin asked with wide eyes.

"Of course, I am," the captain laughed in disbelief at her reaction.

Commander Ashpin went silent for a moment and then sheepishly asked, "So, if I were to carry this locket with me," she paused as Captain Magnus began to frown and gently shake his head, but she continued anyway, "I would have your powers too?"

"I don't want to find out," he said and gently took the locket from her.

"What will you do with it?" she asked as he slipped the locket back into his pocket.

"I'm going to keep it safe until I can trust someone with it," he looked sorrowful, "I hope you understand."

Meeka smiled and gave him a hug, "I'm proud of you," she said and kissed his forehead, "I feel a lot better now, knowing that she's no longer a huge threat."

"She's still dangerous," Captain Magnus warned, "just as dangerous as you are. You had the same teacher."

"I'll keep that in mind," Commander Ashpin smiled and left the bridge.

<hr>

We docked in the Royal dock section of South Port Royale and unloaded our prisoners.

The Royal guards asked if we needed assistance, but we refused and said we had everything under control.

The sun had set about fifteen minutes before we arrived at the castle, so we used the darkness to our advantage and slipped around to the side of the outer courtyard wall.

"This isn't line of sight," Roash complained as the ground team huddled together so Meeka could blink us into the castle.

"Trust me," Meeka whispered, "I know this place fairly well."

"Fairly?" Roash growled as the pink smoke enveloped the team. POP!

We arrived just outside the throne room door and waited a moment for the smoke to fade away.

"I'm surprised we weren't nabbed by guards upon arrival," Navari breathed and woke the bound and gagged prisoners.

Meeka just smiled and pushed the large door open.

The throne room was occupied by the King and his new-to-us wife, the Queen.

The Queen's skin was almost porcelain white and her raven hair made her red lips glow.

The King looked up, as if expecting us and said, "What do we have here?" with a smile, "I heard the pop when you arrived."

"Your Highnesses," Captain Magnus announced with a bow to the Queen, "We have brought you Amaliya and her second in command."

"I've heard of Amaliya," the Queen replied in awe and quickly rose to her feet, "She's older than I expected."

She stood about as tall as the King and was plump to the point of looking as if she may be with child.

No one dared ask.

"She's my mother, Your Highness," Captain Magnus stated.

"How unfortunate," she frowned, "Is it true that she's the leader of the Grand Ascendancy?" the Queen asked, stepping closer.

"It is true, Your Highness," Captain Magnus answered.

The Queen suddenly lunged forward and forcefully slapped Amaliya across the face and spat at her.

The entire room gasped.

"She had my village burned to ashes for no reason," the Queen sobbed with tears welling up in her eyes, "And not only *my* village, but several others around mine."

The King rushed back to her side and embraced her for a long moment, whispering into her ear and rocking her in his arms.

When the Queen was ready, the King let her go and announced, "We will put them in a cell of Avilyn's design," he escorted the Queen back to her throne and sat her down, "a cell even Avilyn himself could not escape."

"Together?" I asked, "My Liege," I added.

"He prepared four cells, in case there were more prisoners," the King reassured.

"Shouldn't we interrogate them now?" Navari asked.

"We should take some time and think of the correct questions before we waste this opportunity," he stated with authority, "Court will be held here in one week," he added and dug into his robe.

He produced five tokens of fiat and handed them to Navari.

As he handed the coins to her, I caught movement behind the Queen.

I looked in just enough time to see Avilyn exit the throne room; it looked like he had been injured and bandaged.

The King dismissed us and we departed back to The Scorpion with a lighter step and a song in our hearts.

The voyage back to the port was delightful, full of laughter and song.

Plans for a party were discussed as the night sounds enveloped us in peace and serenity.

Chapter Sixteen

RESPITE

The realm felt, to us, a bit safer.

We rejoiced and enjoyed ourselves with a quickly put together party as we sailed back to The Scorpion's Den.

The night was warm with a gentle cooling breeze coming from the open sea.

The moon was bright against the cloudless starry sky, reflecting off the water, as shooting stars periodically appeared and disappeared just as quickly.

By the time we left the river, the party was in full bloom.

"Did ye see t'e look on 'er face when Loher popped out in front o' 'er?" Balt laughed and tried to mimic the look.

"I was standing directly behind her when Rion tackled her," Lybiidae giggled, "I had to hit the deck to avoid the collision."

"Yeah, Rion," Captain Magnus added, "what were you *thinking*?"

Rion hung his head and frowned, "Instinct took over," Rion moaned, "I apologize."

"Well, it worked," Captain Magnus smiled, "But next time, follow my orders or someone might get hurt or even killed."

"Aye, Captain," Rion replied and perked up a little.

We sat and enjoyed each other's company for the next few hours, reminiscing over the events of the past few years together; some good, some bad.

We spoke of past companions that we had lost along the way, including Sir Seth Quinn and Byron Le'Abboltt, but the conversation always seemed to return to the same subject of Amaliya and Lemac.

"Now that the mission is almost completed," Commander Ashpin asked, "what are we going to focus on?"

Balt's attention was suddenly piqued, "***Dragons,***" he breathed.

Slight giggles and chuckles trickled through the group.

"The dwarf guessed correctly," Captain Magnus laughed.

"We're going to become dragon slayers?" Ensign Trislee asked with excitement.

"Not *exactly,*" Captain Magnus corrected, "more like, self-appointed guardians of this realm."

"But t'at includes huntin' an' killin' dragons, right?" Balt asked.

"Yes, Balt," Captain Magnus laughed, "if need be, among other things."

Balt, Rion and Trislee smiled at each other with wild eyes.

"We still have the rest of the Grand Ascendancy to take care of," I mentioned.

"I think that should be our main goal for now," Roash suggested.

Captain Magnus smiled and nodded his head.

"Actually," Navari stated, "questions for Amaliya should be the first issue we should take care of."

"Oh, believe me," Captain Magnus added, "I have *plenty* of questions for her."

"As do I," Commander Ashpin replied.

"What will happen to her after she has answered all of our questions?" Nixx asked.

"The Queen seemed pretty angry with her," Lybiidae mentioned, "perhaps the Queen will have her executed."

"My mother or not," Captain Magnus commented, "she deserves to die for what she's done."

"What if they give you the choice?" I asked the captain.

"Then I say hang her," Captain Magnus immediately answered with a sour look on his face.

The bridge fell silent.

Balt suddenly ripped a fart and began to laugh, "T'at's all I's gots ta say about t'at."

Everyone except the poor helmsman exited the bridge, gagging and coughing.

"Nasty, Balt," Loher coughed, "why did you *do* that?"

"WOT?" Balt laughed, "Someone had ta ease t'e tension in t'ere."

The helmsman was still on the bridge, gagging and cursing Balt's name.

The group dispersed and went their separate ways until Balt's stench faded.

I remained near the bridge to keep the helmsman company.

"I've known that dwarf for probably about twenty years now," I began, "why is it now that I discover how truly gross he is?"

The helmsman just frowned, shook his head, and waved the rest of Balt's fumes out of the room.

"May I apologize on behalf of my dwarven companion?" I offered.

"It was bound to happen sooner or later," the helmsman replied with a slight chuckle in his throat.

"The apology?" I asked.

"No," he cracked a smile, "the fart."

I began to chuckle at the oddity of our conversation, leading the helmsman to burst out laughing himself.

About what, I'm unsure.

"Do you enjoy all of this danger?" I asked after our laughter subsided.

"We're safe aboard this ship," he replied soberly, "Do you?"

I chuckled, "I'd be back in Larix by now if I didn't enjoy it a little bit."

"I've never been there," the helmsman chuckled, "I know where it is, but I've never been."

"Humans are usually there by invitation," I stated, "I could show you some time."

"That would be grand," he smiled and tipped his hat.

A few moments of silence passed as we watched the waves pass by along with the time.

The moonlight suddenly darkened as the shape of a large dragon loomed overhead.

Calls of *'Dragon Ho!'* could be heard echoing across the ship as crew members began scurrying around to their stations as fast as they could.

I grabbed my bow and quiver and dashed out to the deck to get a better look.

It was far too dark to make out a color, but the size of this dragon was as big, or perhaps a bit bigger than the one that killed the red dragon a few weeks ago.

Roash stationed herself at the harpoon and began to take aim, awaiting orders from the captain.

Archers of all kinds had also formed in small groups around the ship, standing ready.

Balt, along with his brothers, Ensign Trislee, Rion, and a few other large humans, had gathered at the gang plank, armed to the teeth and ready to finish the job that the harpoon would undoubtedly begin.

The Scorpion suddenly began to glow with the bright blue green glow of a Psi-shield as Captain Magnus strolled out of the bridge and calmly walked amongst his crew.

The dragon circled once, swooped down in front of The Scorpion, and sped away, skimming the water, and disappeared into the darkness.

"DAMMIT!" Balt cursed and pouted himself back down to his quarters, his brothers not far behind.

We kept a lookout in case the dragon decided to make a return, but the hours drifted by with no sightings and The Scorpion finally settled into her cozy cave.

⸺◆⸺

As we entered the lagoon, we encountered a small yacht anchored within.

Several crew members were standing in a group around someone, or something, laughing and enjoying themselves.

"Company?" I asked the room.

"Looks like it," Balt growled.

"A yacht that small couldn't have made it all this way without help," Commander Ashpin pointed out, "I wonder who it is."

"Whoever it is," Captain Magnus laughed and led the way, "seems friendly. Let's find out."

We disembarked and headed toward the group.

"Captain on deck!" a crew member alerted as we walked up.

The crew members all looked at the group of us walking up and cleared a path to our guest.

"I knew you'd be along shortly," Avilyn laughed and reached out his hand.

The old hoary elf looked as if he had been through a rough battle, as the side of his face and down his neck was bandaged, like I thought I had seen the other night in the throne room.

Captain Magnus shook his hand in welcome and asked, teasing, "Vampire?"

Avilyn laughed and answered, "No, I cut myself shaving."

"Seriously," Captain Magnus asked in a serious tone, "what happened?"

Avilyn frowned, "I didn't venture all the way out here to talk about my face."

"Why *are* ye 'ere, Elf?" Balt asked.

"I wish to join the crew," Avilyn said, directly at Balt.

"Really?" Balt and Captain Magnus asked in unison.

"No," he replied emotionlessly.

"Dammit," Captain Magnus cursed under his breath as Balt openly breathed a sigh of relief.

Avilyn laughed and patted the captain on the back.

"I'll ask again, Elf," Balt growled, "why are ye 'ere?"

Avilyn smiled at the dwarf and turned to Captain Magnus, "My informants tell me that there is unusual activity atop Exland mountain."

"W'at dose t'at 'ave ta do wit' us?" Balt asked impatiently. "It has nothing to directly do with you, Balt," Avilyn scowled in an attempt to dismiss the dwarf, "it *does,* however, concern your red haired wizard."

"Commander Ashpin?" Captain Magnus rhetorically asked, "Balt, go fetch Meeka."

"Aye, Captain," Balt grumbled and strolled away.

"Thank you," Avilyn breathed.

"For?" Captain Magnus chuckled.

"The temporary peace I shall enjoy whilst the dwarf has gone away," Avilyn admitted.

"You don't like Balt?" the captain asked.

"I don't particularly care for dwarves in general," Avilyn replied, "too long of a story to get into right now."

A puff of pink smoke began to form about two meters to our right and Meeka appeared from within.

Avilyn smiled at the newcomer, "Master Balt decided not to join you?" he asked, relieved.

"No," she laughed, "he was spouting something about bandages, and now I see why, what happened?"

"He cut himself shaving," Captain Magnus chuckled.

"Kuchoff!" Meeka hissed.

"What?" he asked with a smile, "He said it to me first."

"Now, now children," the elder chuckled, "my face is of no concern right now," he paused, "Ficolus is up to something atop Exland mountain and I sense nothing good from it."

"So why don't you go stop him?" I asked, immediately wishing I hadn't.

The old elf looked at me, "Ficolus and I have a standing treaty to leave each other to our own devices. I cannot interfere."

"Are you not interfering right now," Commander Ashpin asked, "by telling us this?"

"I just want you to take a team and go snooping around," he replied, "and find out what he's doing."

"We have to be in Salvus Hus in two days," Captain Magnus announced, "we're leaving tomorrow. Perhaps we'll take a quick look on our way."

"I think it can wait until you return," Avilyn smiled and began walking back to his yacht.

"Why don't you stay here and return back with us tomorrow?" Commander Ashpin asked as Avilyn blinked back aboard his yacht.

"His Majesty doesn't know I'm gone," Avilyn replied, "I must make haste back to the castle."

With no warning, Avilyn and the entire yacht disappeared in a puff of orange smoke.

The next morning, we woke, had our morning meal, and began our trek back to the castle.

Exland mountain loomed large beside us as we slowly sailed past it.

"Do you see anything strange?" Captain Magnus asked.

"It looks like a mountain to me, Sir," Navari answered as she peered up at the mountain top.

"Nothing unusual though?"

"I used every ocular ability I possess and saw nothing besides an excess bit of heat," she informed, "but Ficolus *lives* up there, so I'm assuming it's from his fireplace."

"Regardless," Commander Ashpin replied, "I'm taking a small team and we're going to go check it out as soon as we return from questioning Amaliya."

"Agreed," Captain Magnus stated.

"Perhaps Amaliya will know what Ficolus is doing up there," I wagered.

"*That* would make things so much easier," Commander Ashpin giggled.

The Scorpion made her way through the Strait of Avilyn, past the harbor and rounded the bend into the river.

The wind was in our favor so we traversed the river in excellent time.

"You're early," the King announced as we disembarked.

"Your Majesties," Captain Magnus bowed as the Royal couple strolled up to us.

"We were just on our evening walk," the Queen mentioned, "join us."

Seeing the Queen up close, her apparent plumpness could now be observed as an obvious pregnancy as she waddled along the pathway back to the castle.

"The prisoners have just been given their evening meal and are secured for the night," the King announced as he helped the Queen step around an unevenness in the path.

"Thank you, My Love," the Queen giggled with a faint curtsy.

"My privilege and honor, My Goddess," the King breathed and bowed to her.

Loher nudged me in the ribs with her elbow and smiled.

We continued on our way.

"They haven't given you any problems, have they?" Captain Magnus asked.

"Not in the slightest," the King smiled, "as a matter of fact, the guards tell me that Amaliya is quite charming and comedic."

Captain Magnus raised a questioning eyebrow at the King but decided to stay silent.

"And the other?" Loher asked.

"Lemac?" the King laughed, "He's a nasty one. Keeps threatening death on whoever he speaks to."

We entered the castle and proceeded to the guest quarters.

"May I presume our normal rooms are available?" Meeka asked.

"They are," the King replied, "we have no guests tonight besides yourselves, so they're all available."

Navari shuffled her feet, seeming a bit nervous.

"Is something wrong, my Dear?" the Queen asked.

"I- I've never slept in a castle before," Navari shyly announced.

The Queen smiled at her, trying to relax her guest.

Meeka gently grabbed her by the arm and said, "We can bunk together."

"Don't do it," Roash chuckled, "she snores."

"I don't snore," Meeka giggled, "I purr."

Captain Magnus rolled his eyes and laughed loudly.

"No you don't," Roash laughed, "I purr, you *snore.*"

Navari began to laugh.

"You can have your own room," the Queen laughed, enjoying the playful banter.

"Or you can bunk with me and Euka," Lybiidae offered, "we don't snore or purr."

"I purr a little," Euka qualified, "but I cuddle and that should make up for it."

The Royal couple were shocked and amused at the sight of a speaking caracal.

"What *wonderful* magic!" the Queen breathed in awe.

"You've only just begun to see the wonders this realm has to offer," the King said sweetly and kissed her cheek.

Navari accepted the Drow's offer and we settled in for the night.

⸻ ❈ ⸻

We awoke the next morning and rejoined in the dining room for a breakfast literally served on silver platters.

"The prisoners will be ready as soon as they've finished their breakfasts," a guard announced as the King and Queen entered and joined us in our meal.

"May I ask what will be done with the prisoners once we're done questioning them?" Meeka asked.

"That depends on the answers they give," the King answered between bites.

Captain Magnus looked up with a worried look on his face, "So, you might let them live?"

"It's possible," the King laughed, "do you *want* them to die?"

"Yes," Captain Magnus replied with no hesitation.

The Queen smiled and continued eating.

"Tell me why," the King politely ordered, setting down his fork.

"Murder," Captain Magnus stated, "she has killed so many people," he said, "including my father indirectly, my neighbors, *her* neighbors," gesturing toward the Queen...

"Don't forget Byron," Commander Ashpin added.

"And hundreds of eline," Roash added as well.

"I understand," the King held up a hand, "Is there anything else?"

There was a slight moment of silence as we looked at each other, thinking.

"***Dragons***..." Balt breathed.

The Queen coughed in surprise, almost choking on the bit of food she was chewing.

She had a frightened look on her face as she looked at Balt, "You can't be serious."

"I'm afraid the dwarf is being deadly serious," Avilyn announced as he walked into the room, "Majesties."

"How is Amaliya to blame for the dragons?" the King asked, visibly shaken.

"She has been using a portal to other realms," Commander Ashpin explained the best she could, "Apparently, she found a realm that supports dragons and she took a few eggs."

The King looked at Avilyn for confirmation and the old hoary elf nodded affirmation.

"We already killt a green one an' a red one," Balt proudly commented.

Avilyn suddenly looked hurt in a strange way upon hearing the news.

"Actually," Roash corrected, "it was that giant iridescent one that killed the red one."

Avilyn began to smile at that news.

"How did *that one* die?" the King asked with wide eyes.

"After killing the red dragon, it didn't attack us, so we let it go and followed it into another realm," Captain Magnus answered.

"Which realm did you arrive in?" Avilyn asked, quite interested.

Commander Ashpin stood up and began describing the scene with her hands and body language, "It was a beautiful, forested area with a gentle river flowing through it."

Avilyn sat down and grabbed a handful of bacon.

"With pine trees everywhere," Roash added.

Avilyn began to chew on a chunk of bacon, seemingly uninterested in the answer, but the royal couple were on the edge of their seats, paying absolute attention.

When Avilyn didn't respond, the King took the initiative and asked, "Did you talk to anyone?"

I nodded my head and began to speak, but the King continued by asking, "Do they speak our language?"

"Yes, my Liege," I answered, "they speak our language as well."

"At least the few we talked to do," Captain Magnus added.

"What were they like?" the Queen asked.

"Flamboyant," I laughed, "larger than life."

"Giants?" the King asked with wider eyes.

"No," I chuckled, "they use grand gestures," I explained, gesturing grandly, "and they speak *with song in their voices,*" I sang.

Captain Magnus began to laugh and nodded his head, "Exactly like that," he chuckled in amusement.

The royal couple were laughing along, genuinely amused by the story.

"When we arrived back to Beornan Heafod," Captain Magnus continued soberly, "Amaliya was waiting for us and attacked us without warning."

"We defended ourselves and captured Amaliya and Lemac," I completed.

"Speaking of which," the King said, wiping the corner of his mouth and rising from his chair, "the prisoners should be ready by now."

He assisted the Queen to her feet and kissed her on the cheek, "You don't have to join us if you don't want to," he said.

"I'd rather not," she replied and glanced fearfully at Navari, "I think I'll stay here."

Navari bowed to the Queen and replied, "I take no offence, Your Majesty."

"I'm glad you understand," the Queen smiled, sat back down, and took a sip from her cup.

"My Love," the King bowed and led us out of the room, leaving the Queen to finish her breakfast in peace.

— ◆ —

"This should prove to be interesting," Captain Magnus stated as we began to climb the stairs to the dungeon tower.

"I always thought dungeons were underground," I commented.

"From what I understand," the King began, "my great, great, great, grandfather built the dungeon high enough that the fall would be instant death instead of underground where it's been proven tunneling is a potential escape option."

Commander Ashpin looked out of the window and down to the ground, "Even *I* wouldn't attempt a 'blink' to the ground from here, and we're not even to the dungeon yet."

"Why not?" Loher asked, "It's line of sight."

"It's difficult to determine the correct distance and you may end up blinking into the ground," Commander Ashpin answered, "besides, those thorn bushes would tear you to ribbons."

"You're correct," the King laughed, "Avilyn told me that he planted those thorn bushes down there for precisely that reason," the King informed, "I believe that's why he's all bandaged up, but he won't talk about it."

"That makes sense," Captain Magnus laughed.

We arrived at the top of the tower where the dungeon began.

"Where are the guards that are supposed to be stationed here?" the King rhetorically asked.

The hallway to the dungeon area was empty.

We began to walk to the dungeon door when we suddenly heard the sounds of swordplay.

The King tried to push open the dungeon door, but it wouldn't budge.

Balt, Captain Magnus, and I attempted to help him push, but even with our combined weight and strength, the door would not move.

"Stand back," Captain Magnus warned and began to summon up Psi energy.

"Psi-Time," Balt chuckled and braced for whatever was coming next.

Captain Magnus reached back with both hands as if he were holding something in his hands above his head, and then lunged forward, throwing the Psi-energy directly through the door, splintering it into hundreds of smaller shards.

He drew his katana and rushed into the room.

Balt was right behind him, howling out a battle cry.

EPILOGUE

I quickly followed my companions into the dungeon and saw Lemac sword fighting with two royal guards.

Two other guards lay dead on the floor, along with Amaliya still in her cell; smoke was emanating from her corpse, yet she didn't look like she had been burned.

Lemac, fighting two well trained royal guards, was holding his own quite nicely as he was using both fallen guards' swords at the same time.

The guards were trying their best but seemed to continue to come up short.

Lemac suddenly screamed out a wild cry as he dropped the sword from his right hand and shot lightning out of his palm.

The guard to his left began to twitch violently, dropping his weapon and then falling to the ground in a smoking heap.

Shaken and confused, the guard to Lemac's right was easily neutralized as Lemac ran his sword through the guard's neck and pushed hard, partially decapitating him.

Then, with a puff of black smoke, Lemac suddenly disappeared.

"Dammit!" Balt growled and stomped his foot on the floor.

Commander Ashpin ran to the closest window and looked out, "Well," she said as we all joined her by the window, "The Exland Mountain mystery has just been solved," she pointed out the window.

We looked and observed a cloud of black smoke disappearing just behind another green dragon, soaring around the castle.

Ficolus and Lemac were on the green dragon's back, flying away.

We watched as they disappeared over the horizon in the direction of The Haze.

I turned to look at Captain Magnus and found him sitting crossed legged on the floor, cradling the head of his deceased mother in his lap, crying.

"Leave him be," Loher whispered.

Commander Ashpin and I nodded and I gazed out of the window, wondering what our next move was going to be.

Now that the Grand Ascendancy was under Lemac's control, they seemed like an even *larger* threat than it did when Amaliya was involved.

Her limited protection over Captain Kuchoff Magnus was gone and he was no longer safe.

We had to be ready.

If you enjoyed **Cove** please post a review
and watch for Book Five of The Scorpion Chronicles.
Coming soon...

www.ingramcontent.com/pod-product-compliance
Lightning Source LLC
Chambersburg PA
CBHW032031310726
48972CB00002B/622